The Parish

By Todd Downing

FIRST EDITION

ISBN: 979-8-9861181-5-4

Edited by Raechelle Downing
Cover design by Todd Downing

WWW.TODDDOWNING.COM

Mute Angst Envy – *The Sword and the Cross*
(St. Thomas / Holmes / Zimmerman)
© ® Kitchen Whore Music / BMI

Lyrics used by permission

Deep7 Press is a subsidiary of Despot Media, LLC
1214 Woods Rd SE Port Orchard, WA 98366 USA
WWW.DEEP7.COM

For those who have lost,
For those who grieve...
It doesn't get easier,
but if you do the work,
your heart will get bigger.

No way out but through.

Foreword

This doesn't usually happen.

Normally a book is released, studios and production companies acquire the film rights, and a film is adapted from the original source material.

On the rare occasion, the author of the original book adapts the work for the screenplay. Ray Bradbury is a famous example of this in regard to *Something Wicked This Way Comes.*

And then sometimes an original screenplay —say, *Star Wars*—is novelized by an author for hire—say, Alan Dean Foster.

But sometimes, a writer has spent a good chunk of time toiling in the screenplay form, thus the script is written first, then novelized for the book market. For better or worse, that's been my modus operandi for most of my career. Writing for the stage, screen, audiodrama, and comic book page has given me a modicum of skill with dialog and story, and I've parlayed that into long-form narrative.

In the 2010s, when I was very active in the Seattle independent film community, I happened to write three horror screenplays which were seemingly unconnected except by familiar geography and the fact that they were female-driven. I tend to "head cast" from the talent pool I interact with, and the middle script of the three was written with a specific actress friend in mind. Drawing partly on some "creepy things kids say" memes and partly on grief and the horrors of war, the screenplay for *The Parish* was written in early 2014, and we began to make the rounds, pitching it to various investors and production companies. At some point in 2018, an angel investor ponied up most of the funds. It was shot in the fall of 2018 and, because of some post production audio issues and COVID, didn't see official release until 2020.

It's hard to be objective with a film I've been closely tied to from the beginning, despite multiple attempts at divorcing my ego from the final product. There are so many strikes against indie films right out of the gate. It's an intimate, Washington-made film, produced for less than half a million dollars. It stars little-known Pacific Northwest talent, save for horror icon Bill Oberst Jr. But it's beautifully-shot, emotionally engaging, with good performances. The fact that it got made at all, much less secured worldwide distribution without major stars or a huge budget is a real achievement. I remain proud of that.

Even so, there was always going to be more story to tell. At over twenty drafts of the script. a lot of character development and backstory would never be seen in the final film. I wanted to put all of that on the page, and do the same for the other two stories in the "trilogy". The characters deserved that much.

So that's why this book is coming out after —and based on—the screenplay. That's why some of this narrative departs from the events of the film. It's a totally different animal and should be considered as such.

Rewind to the summer of 2014. We were preparing to move west across Puget Sound to the Kitsap Peninsula, where we'd fallen in love with a craftsman home on five acres in the woods. While my wife Raechelle packed and prepped for the sale of our West Seattle home, I commuted east over the mountains to Ellensburg to work production design on the indie Sasquatch movie *Hunting Grounds*. After several weeks driving from Seattle to Ellensburg to Kitsap to Seattle (rinse and repeat), I wrapped on the Bigfoot movie and we finally packed up our two cats, our elderly German shepherd, and our college age daughter, and retreated to our new home in the sticks.

It was dark when we arrived, the local coyotes singing us a welcome as we unloaded a few basics. That haunting chorus really sold me on the new digs, and I began to explore the history of this peninsula, named for a Suquamish chief. I began to see the potential to add external drama to my contemporary horror stories through the bloody history of the place. The die was cast.

Welcome to Slaughter County.

- Todd Downing, Port Orchard, WA
Summer, 2021

Acknowledgments

Thanks to Keith St. Thomas of Mute Angst Envy for the use of the lyrics from *The Sword and the Cross*. Thanks also to Paul Zimmerman, and Jack Robert Holmes (rest in peace), for making some great music over the years. *facebook.com/muteangstenvy*

Thanks to Raffael Boccamazzo, PhD, aka Dr. B, for his kind participation in helping me craft the behaviors and complex psyches of these characters. *takethis.org*

Thanks to Ryan Fisher and Brian Meredith for letting me mention their indie comic book properties. Fisher's *Torchlight Lullaby* is especially required reading.

Thanks to Jason Yarnell and Bravo Company, 1st Tiger Brigade, 3/67, 2nd

Armored Division ("Hounds of Hell") for their stories and the willingness to share them.

Thanks to my friends Angela and David at Mighty Tripod Productions, for taking on the film, and returning the novel rights. Special thanks to Bill Oberst Jr. for inhabiting the character of Father Felix so well on-screen.

The byline of the quoted *Psychology Today* article actually belongs to Frank T. McAndrew, PhD.

The inspiration for Father Felix was a bald bulldog of a priest at St. Francis Middle School in Watsonville, California in the late '70s, before it became a high school. Like his fictional counterpart, he was an Army veteran, and also presided at the affiliated summer camp. The boys at the school bestowed the nickname "Fifi" on him, of which he was none too fond.

The inspiration for Liz and Audrey was the real life experience of losing my wife to cancer and being rudderless on the sea of grief while trying to raise two school-age children.

CR

Don't you cry for me
Never fear
The sword and cross in my hands
Angels appear

- Mute Angst Envy

CHAPTER 1

Kandahar, 2018.

Chaos in slow motion.

The air around the blast site swirled and billowed, choked with brick dust and toxic gray smoke. Screams of children and schoolteachers, some still half-buried in rubble, wove a morbid tapestry of sound, saturating everything in the district. Sound that sat heavy on the city, almost crushing it. Sound so thick it was only cut by the wail of emergency sirens, a high-pitched ringing, and labored breathing.

Captain Jason Charles staggered through the carcass of the school, dun combat boots caked dusty white, his desert-camo Marine Corps uniform strangely undamaged. The bill of a matching utility cap sat low across bloodshot chestnut eyes. He was chiseled, wiry. A dark, sunbaked complexion and monolid eyes spoke of Filipino extraction. His angular jaw was stippled with soot and ash, high cheek-bones striped red with weeping abrasions.

The limp body of an unconscious Afghan boy lay like a sack of flour in the Captain's arms. The child's only crime had been sitting in school when the IED detonated.

Boots scuffed and wobbled over a hellish avalanche of brick, stone and mortar, of electrical wires and the occasional jagged timber. Random limbs—mostly those of children—scattered the area. To the Captain's left, a sandal with the foot still in it, a shard of jagged bone winking from the center of the rent flesh. To the right, a child's *Chitrali* cap, spattered with blood and brain matter. One tiny arm clad in charred rags extended from a pile of debris, seemingly pointing the way out.

Captain Charles turned, following the dead finger as he scanned the muffled blanket of sound for an emergency siren. Help was coming. He just needed to get the boy in his arms out of the blast zone to a safe location.

2:47 p.m.

1447 military time.

Once again, the Marine's boot came down on a pile of debris. He could have stepped in any of a thousand places in this bombed-out school. Literally anywhere else would have been safer. But this particular pile of debris covered a secondary IED.

The world went black as the blast ripped through him.

He awoke in a haze, the stench of burning flesh and hair heavy around him. He'd landed in an almost sitting position, propped against a pile of charred masonry and wooden pallets, about twenty paces back from the fateful footstep. Through blurry, blood-streaked vision, he could make out a wet mass of entrails and viscera below his chest, stretching over the bricks and beneath his line of sight.

The Afghan boy was nowhere to be seen.

Nor was Jason Charles' lower half.

The skin on his left hand and face had been transformed to the look and consistency of raw hamburger. His right arm was gone. Pain receptors vacillated between a dull throb and complete screaming overload.

For the first time, he noticed the silence. It was absolutely, horrifically silent. Not even so much as the familiar piercing tone so common after experiencing a close-proximity blast.

He knew at that moment that the only reason he was conscious and aware was that his brain hadn't informed the rest of his body that it was dead.

Captain Jason Charles lay torn in half on a blood-soaked pile of bricks in Kandahar, slowly dying over the course of three and a half minutes. He tried calling out, but only vomited blood. Unable to do anything but feel his life slip from him, he thought of his wife and daughter back in San Diego before darkness overtook his vision and the world saturated back to white.

CB

Sunday.

Day zero.

Liz Charles awoke with a sudden gasp for breath. Blinking feverishly, she struggled to gather her bearings, and the pieces eventually locked into place.

She found herself sitting behind the wheel of the family Jeep Grand Cherokee, parked at an Interstate 5 rest stop just north of Olympia. It had been a marathon road trip up the West Coast from San Diego, but they were close now.

Glancing in the side mirror, she saw the haggard face of a single mother in her early forties. Red-rimmed green eyes stared back from sockets that alternated between sunken and puffy, depending on how much crying she'd been doing. A stray lock of dark walnut hair, now highlighted with silver—at no extra charge—hung across her cheek. In a single, graceful motion, she brushed it back over the top of her ear, tucking it into a royal blue bandanna with the rest. Her thick mane had once been a stylish bob cut, but had grown down to her shoulders, unkempt and lifeless.

Liz looked down and noticed the front of the gray crew neck sweatshirt was streaked with grease spots and mustard stains. It was evidence of a thousand miles driven, of meals eaten behind the wheel, without a solid night's sleep, without a shower, and without a change of clothes.

She frowned. This was Jase's favorite sweatshirt.

Sighing, she reassured herself that she could always wash it when they arrived. But then the thought occurred that it didn't matter, ultimately. After all, it wasn't like he was going to need it back.

A gentle rain played down the windshield in thin rivulets, causing a slow, gray cascade of refracted light to wash over the silver crucifix that dangled from the rear view mirror. A USMC anchor sticker in the left corner of the rear window balanced the yellow ribbon decal in the right, proclaiming the Charles family's support for "the troops".

A sudden tap on the passenger window jolted her upright in her seat. She turned to meet a pair of dark eyes glaring at her from outside. They were Jase's eyes. Her husband's eyes. But they peered at her from the face of her daughter.

Liz blinked, and the girl pointed at the passenger door lock.

Shaking loose the cobwebs from her head, Liz triggered the automatic lock from the driver's side door, and Audrey Charles slid into the passenger seat, hair matted with the misty rain.

She threw Liz a look of disbelief. "Really?"

Audrey was eleven going on twenty, with her Filipino father's chestnut eyes and her Italian mother's dark hair, but a complexion shades lighter than either of them. A pair of earbuds lay across her shoulder, running down to the iPod in the pocket of her black hoodie.

"Sorry," Liz offered. "You good for a while?"

Audrey didn't answer, simply regarding Liz for an awkward moment before looking away. "Fall asleep again?"

Liz turned the key in the ignition, urging the Jeep back to life. "I'm fine," she said. "We're almost there."

Audrey shot her another sarcastic look. "That's what you said back in Oregon." She replaced the earbuds as Liz backed out of the parking spot, and the family Jeep found the freeway on-ramp once again.

A gray blanket of overcast sky hung suspended over a gray highway, which bisected a gray patchwork of farmland and industry. Despite the presence of lush forests and magnificent waterways, gray was the constant, more than any single color or shade. It permeated everything, from vistas to moods, like a basement window once mildew has taken hold.

North of Tacoma, they took Highway 16 across the Narrows, onto a peninsula nestled in the crotch of Puget Sound. It was hilly and wet, and shaped like a devil's tail, bitten and scarred with a million creeks and tributaries. The suffering of generations of native people was written on the landscape and wafted through every fog bank.

Audrey shivered. She just knew people had died here. So many people.

The land screamed it.

Eventually their exit appeared and they followed the signs into a small, rural community where time had apparently stopped during the Kennedy administration. Local townsfolk ambled to and fro on their way nowhere important, to do nothing in particular. Mom and pop shop fronts and nineteenth century western facades spoke to a community not yet swallowed by urban sprawl.

The only hint that the 21st century was truly in swing was that about half of the commercial space was vacant, with FOR LEASE signs as plentiful as coffee shops and junk stores—quaintly referred to as "antique malls".

The black Jeep pulled to a stop at what was probably the only traffic light in town, and a small group of people made use of the crosswalk, its paint long worn away. Liz glanced to her left, finding the steeple of a church several blocks away, down a side street. On the main strip, a bearded mail carrier in his fifties, clad in Postal Service jacket and cap, exited the candy shop and headed next door to the frame store.

"It's green."

Liz startled, shifting her gaze back to the traffic signal. She'd missed the light change. "Ah, yeah."

A few more blocks and a turn off the main street took them into a neighborhood of craftsman bungalows and Tudor cottages. Semi-rural suburbia. Civilization without sidewalks. The skinny townhomes of brogrammers and yuppies had not yet invaded. The middle class had not yet died here.

As they continued down a sleepy street lined with maples beginning to change color, the small Catholic church she'd seen from the traffic light became more visible. It sat on the crest of the hill, parochial school on the opposite side of the street, comprised of a century-old brick building and blacktop play area. The church itself was a simple, no-nonsense affair, dating from the same era as the school, and constructed of the same early 20th century red brick. An equally simple cross sprouted from the top of the steeple, pointing into the sky.

Audrey leaned her head against the passenger window, tinny music blaring from her earbuds. Taking in the school and noting the empty jungle gym and unoccupied tether ball poles, she realized this was probably where her mom had registered her.

The notion wasn't particularly bothersome. She was a veteran of private Catholic schools. It was far from her first rodeo. She just hoped that whatever crisis her mom was navigating, whatever this was, would come to a conclusion soon, so they could return home to San Diego, where their support network was. Where grandma and grandpa were. Where her friends were.

Where the sun was.

CHAPTER 2

Liz pulled the Jeep to a final stop in front of an old brick Tudor cottage. The picket fence surrounding the front yard was badly in need of paint, and the arbor across the front path had never been painted in the first place. It was draped in the dead tendrils of morning glory and climbing roses in September.

The Mitchell Group real estate sign boasted SOLD by an agent named SANDRA CAS-SIDY. Her photo was every realtor headshot from the beginning of time, including the air-brushed makeup and coiffed blond cascade of hair.

Liz and Audrey stared from the front of the car.

"Is that the new house?" Audrey asked, putting down the passenger window to better see the front of the place, with its three-step concrete walk up, door light with a decorative spindle missing, and the bay window in the dining room to the left. A larger picture window to the right glared out across the dead lawn, looking like a giant baleful eye.

"Yep," Liz answered, taking a sip from the water bottle in the console.

"I liked our old one."

Liz noticed someone exiting through the front door and tried to change the subject. "There's Sandra, the realtor," she said, opening the driver's side door. "She'll have our keys."

Sandra was in her 40s and a dead ringer for her photo on the sign. Tall and generously curvy, she looked like a St. Pauli Girl beer logo. She was fashionably dressed and slathered in makeup, her smile looking less like it was forced and more like it had just been killed on the battlefield and rigor mortis had set in. Her black overcoat hid a leopard print blouse and leather skirt from her late 20s which spoke of poor choices and a poorer recollection of having made them.

"Hi hi!" she sang, almost skipping down the front stoop and ducking through the arbor. Her personality was the human equivalent of a venti quad-shot latte.

Audrey slid from the passenger seat and silently pulled the earbuds from her head, wadding them into the pocket of her sweatshirt. She watched her mom greet the new woman with an awkward embrace over a basket of "welcome" gifts for their new abode: scented candles, a dish towel embroidered with a cartoon dog, and a bottle of wine.

"Sandra," Liz fawned with a half-smile. "Thanks so much for meeting us. I hope we didn't keep you waiting."

Sandra grasped Liz by the shoulders, having mysteriously transferred the gift basket to her. "Not at all! Not at all! Just giving the place a little tidy before you got here."

Liz nodded politely without replying.

An awkward pause descended on the three, and Sandra looked as though the pain of silence was excruciating. "Well! Would you like to check out your new house?" she asked finally, shaking her frosted blond head toward the front door.

Audrey shrugged.

Sandra looked from the shy girl back to her mother, who forced a smile.

"Okay! Good! Right this way, ladies!"

A brisk autumn breeze gave way to the stuffy interior of the remodeled 1920s cottage. White plaster walls and dark wood trim were the hallmarks of the architecture named for the British monarchy most associated with the look. A quaint living room was centered around a brick fireplace, and led into a tiny formal dining area and square kitchen. An oak staircase meandered up to the second floor and the bedrooms.

Furniture and boxes were piled everywhere. Liz noted that her labeling system appeared to have worked. The boxes in the living room were actually marked LIVING ROOM.

"I see the truck got here," she said.

"Yes, I just had them go by your labeling system and move everything in. Very thorough, Liz."

"I get it from my mom."

Sandra's brow furrowed as if caught on a breakwater. "Get what?"

"The organizing gene," Liz explained.

Sandra's rigor mortis smile returned. "Well I could use you in my office. If you ever need work, when the benefits run out..." She heard the words as they tumbled from her mouth, unable to stop them. Backpedaling as best she could to salvage the situation, she added, "I'm so sorry to bring that up. Oh God, Liz."

Liz shot Sandra a weary look. "It's alright."

Audrey stood to the side of the door, surveying the interior with a blank face. She could tell Sandra genuinely wanted to be helpful, but that was Sandra's deal—not hers. It wasn't in Audrey's job description to heal the uncomfortable silences.

"Audrey?" The realtor smile reappeared with a vengeance. "Did your mom mention we went to college together?"

Audrey sighed, and wandered off to explore her new surroundings, leaving Liz with another uncomfortable silence to apologize for.

"I'm sorry, Sandra, she's just..."

"Oh, not at all, Liz. It's totally understandable with all you've been through. If there's anything I can do..."

Liz managed a smile, although it took every ounce of emotional strength she could muster. "You can show us around our new house we've only seen in photos."

Crisis averted. The vivacious color returned to Sandra's cheeks as she gestured through the dining room. "Yes, of course. Let's look at the kitchen. The previous owners made some lovely updates..."

╋

Long, awkward silences were nothing new to Liz and Audrey. Each had her own issues to explore internally, and required the emotional space to do it. Liz, now in her forties, widowed and raising a pre-teen girl on her own. Audrey, just hitting the chemical rollercoaster of adolescence, a daddy's girl robbed of the parent she most identified with. They were becoming seasoned experts at silence. They spoke it fluently.

It was no surprise that the two now sat mere feet from one another across an old family table in the dining room, each staring blankly into infinity. Both picked at plates of takeout Chinese food, greasy cardboard containers forming a wall between them. A bottle of Not My Circus "Big Top Red Blend" table wine sat half-empty to Liz's left, next to a large goblet containing a healthy pour. Audrey still had her earbuds in, the acoustic rasp and kick drum of "Two Coffins" by Against Me! spilling into the space between them.

Liz was already tipsy, and Audrey reckoned she couldn't put off the big question any longer.

"Mom?"

Liz signaled for her daughter to set aside the mobile phone and remove her earbuds, and Audrey complied.

"Yes?" Liz blinked with a smile.

Audrey hesitated, but then: "Do I have to go to school tomorrow?"

"Yes," Liz answered with a slight chuckle, inferring how silly the question was.

"Can't I stay home a day? Just to unpack and settle in?"

"It's really best if you don't miss any more school..."

At that moment, Audrey's voice took a particular tone. A tone which told Liz she was in for a fight. A fight no one would win. "But it's a *brand* new house. And a *brand* new town. Just *one day?*"

Liz took a hard swallow of the cheap vintage. "No buts, young lady. No 'just ones'. We were lucky to get you in at St. Francis."

Audrey scowled, pushed her plate away and folded her arms in disgust. "I hate it here."

Liz threw her a motherly yet impatient look. "How can you say that? We just got here. Like literally four hours ago."

"Why can't we just live with Grandma and Grandpa? They always knew what to do..."

"And you're saying I don't?"

Audrey leveled a sideways glance at her mother. No retort necessary.

Liz turned her demeanor from combative to sarcastic, breaking the tension. "Why, child, I carried you in my belly for nine whole months —"

"Uterus," the twelve-year-old corrected.

Liz paused, caught off-guard by Audrey's frank use of proper medical terminology. "I... yes, my uterus. Was where I carried you."

"Babies don't gestate in the stomach," Audrey repeated from some rudimentary sex education text, adding her own snark for good measure.

Liz's response was clipped and scattered as she tried to make three points at once. "What —no, no they don't—but 'belly' is a general term for the whole area—*and* that means I know you better than anyone. And I know what you need right this very minute." She tossed a wrapped fortune cookie over the wall of take-out boxes, and it landed on Audrey's plate. "Fortune cookies for all!"

Audrey let her solemn facade fall and indulged a giggle, responding dramatically to her mom's sarcastic play. "For me? Oh, *thank you*, Mother."

"Go ahead, open it," Liz nodded, almost slurring now almost through her third glass of wine. "See what your future holds."

The Charles women tore into the cellophane wrapping to extract their cookies, cracking them open to get at the message inside.

Audrey was immediately unimpressed. "So stupid."

"Come on, party pooper," Liz chided, reading her own tiny slip of paper and stifling a chuckle.

"What is it?"

"Apparently I will meet a tall stranger."

Audrey cast a dubious side-eye across the take-out barrier. "Whaaaat?"

"I know! In town for less than a day, and already the fortune cookies are trying to set me up on a date."

"That's a lame fortune."

Uncomfortable with the suggestion of romance, Liz deflected back to her daughter. "Well what's yours? Any better?"

Audrey read aloud, puzzling over the meaning as she did so. "Hidden secrets will be revealed to you."

Liz and Audrey shared a look, simultaneously bursting out in laughter.

"Yeah, like how to cooperate with your mother…"

"Or who let that fart…"

"What?" Liz looked surprised, eventually smelling the gift her daughter had left.

Audrey stood, backing away with her dinner plate. "May I be excused?"

"Wha-—?? You little—Ugh! How do you make that smell so bad??" Liz lapsed between laughter and shock at Audrey's brazen stunt.

Audrey carried her plate into the kitchen. "Chinese food!"

"It doesn't work that fast!" Liz protested with another large swig of wine.

Audrey reemerged from the kitchen and headed for the stairs, grinning. "I'm gonna unpack my room!"

Liz slouched in her chair, hailing after her daughter. "Don't forget to take a shower tonight, young lady! You smell like a thousand miles of hard road…and farts!" She shook her head, sighing to herself, "You are your father's daughter, I swear."

Lifting the wine glass to her lips, she gulped down the last bit and reached for the bottle to refresh it, reconsidering at the last moment. She set down the bottle and relaxed in the quiet room, closing her eyes and centering herself. After a few moments, she opened them and began to tidy the table from her seat, picking up the fortunes and looking at them once more.

YOU WILL MEET A TALL STRANGER

Straightening the slips of paper in front of her, she flashed an enigmatic look and grabbed the bottle again, following through on the refill.

It was going to take a lot of wine to get through this.

CHAPTER 3

The scrape of boots on shattered cinderblock in the darkness.

Imagination was so much worse than actually being there. Sometimes, Liz's mental "video" was clear and crisp, like a virgin film print in a quality theater. Sometimes, it was grainy, glitchy, like a worn VHS tape. It became especially so when her mind wandered away from the known facts and into that realm of imagination, where her brain would fill in the gaps, inventing a new level of horror for her to dream...

Again, and again.

Every night, self-medicated with wine and a selection of sleeping pills or anti-anxiety meds, Liz dreamed the same timeline of events. It always started in the dark, just after the first IED. Gradually the scene would fade in, just like a movie. Jason would stumble through the loose bricks and rubble, the young Afghan boy in his arms. Sometimes she would see his boot in close-up, stepping on the second explosive device, and she'd try to scream a warning. But a combination of her soporific cocktail and sleep paralysis put a stop to her effecting any alteration of the outcome.

It always ended with Jase lying in pieces on that blood-soaked pile of bricks and wood pallets, his hamburger face a grotesque, unrecognizable Halloween mask. A far cry from the handsome man she'd married, and made a child with.

And just as always, as her dream vision hovered close over that horrible, charred face, his eyes flashed open, bloodshot and intense and full of fear. He reached for her with his remaining hand, trying to speak but only spewing blood from a throat which channeled no air. Suddenly everything saturated white and the dream crashed in on itself with an unnatural shriek.

Liz gasped for her own air as she shot upright in bed, clawing at the sheets as she tried not to fall off the edge of the world.

"Jase!" escaped in a hiss through dry lips.

It took a few moments of terrified breaths to recalibrate, recalling where she was and the fact that, no matter what she imagined, her husband was still dead. There would always be one less occupied seat at the dinner table. Her daughter would grow up without a father.

And she was still alone. Alone, and angry at any god that would take such a good man from the world...from his family. Shaken in her faith. Shaken in her heart. Shaken in her very foundation.

The room was quiet and dark, unlived-in. Moving boxes lined the walls and corners. An antique oval mirror in the corner reflected the diffuse glow from a streetlight outside. A lone nightstand with bedside lamp and red digital clock sat next to a queen-size bed far too large for a single person.

Liz glanced around the room, gathering her bearings. She picked up the framed family photo from the nightstand—the trip to New York City the summer before Jase shipped out on what would be his last tour of duty. It was a selfie of the happy trio on the observation deck of the Empire State Building, with the sprawl of Manhattan below. Her eyes immediately welled with tears.

Replacing the photo on its kickstand, she glanced at the clock—3:17 a.m.

She always awoke at 3:17 a.m. Jase had died at about 2:47 p.m. Kandahar time, so it made sense to Liz that her brain would replay the moment their bond, their emotional lifeline, was severed.

Taking a deep breath, she opened the nightstand drawer, revealing a family Bible, some random elastic hairbands, and a couple of prescription bottles. Her left hand caressed the leather-bound cover of the holy book, but ultimately opted for the pills. Opening one of the containers, she popped two of whatever was inside, washing it down with a small glass of water. She replaced the bottle in the drawer and shut it with a quiet *thump*, rolling over into the fetal position to eke out another couple hours of sleep.

Sleep now. Confession later.

◯

Day one.

St. Francis School was an oddity. Built in 1903 of cheap brick and shrewd political maneuvering, it was a beacon of the Franciscan Order in a sea of Jesuit institutions. Spanish

Franciscan monks had established the mission system up the California coast in the 1700s, their influence dwindling into the Oregon Territory. It was unusual—though certainly not unheard of—to find a Franciscan community like this one, so far north.

The church sat on the uphill side of a maple-lined street from the school, modest by most comparisons. Unlike the coastal missions of adobe brick and whitewashed stucco, St. Francis Church was built of that same cheap brick, with dark wood accents. It had a remarkably Old World feel, almost as if it had been transported from a Medieval backwater somewhere in Eastern Europe. There was very little of the gold and the guilt of the Vatican. Just simple craftsmanship to create an intercom to God.

St. Francis School was originally intended to serve children of all educational levels, yet at various times over the previous century, the local population had outgrown capacity. High school and elementary kids were reassigned to other facilities, leaving St. Francis a small but respected middle school of 6th, 7th and 8th grades.

It smelled musty, as most old buildings do. But there was something else about the old brick schoolhouse that Audrey sensed as they entered through the double doors. It was a similar feeling to the one she'd had as they were driving into this wet, moss-covered county. A sensation of re-living history, as if playing an old film reel through one of those old Bell & Howell classroom projectors. But instead of a lecture on plutonic rock formations and erosion, it was death captured on that old, grainy film. Every indigenous village razed to the ground by the U.S. Army, every native scalp or head taken as a bounty, every lynching, every murder...the weight of it all seemed to permeate every last inch of the place.

Audrey frowned. She knew enough American history to understand the indigenous genocide that had transpired since the founding of the country, and the brutality which still persisted any time mineral wealth or oil was discovered on Indian land. She knew atrocities had occurred all over the nation, from sea to shining sea. Surely this place was no different.

Surely it hadn't borne witness to *more* than the usual obscene amount of death.

And why would she feel this strange, gloomy foreboding within the walls of a school?

A ringing school bell signaled the beginning of class. The halls echoed with the bustle of lockers and backpacks, sneakers on linoleum, and students reconnecting after the weekend.

A well-dressed woman met them as they passed the office. Faye Phillips was in her forties, of mixed ethnicity, with a dark complexion and raven hair pinned back in a professional bun. She seemed like a serious person with a bubbly facade, which was kind of par for the course in this town.

Audrey was vaguely aware of some pleasantries exchanged between the woman and her mom.

"So glad to finally get to meet you, Mrs. Charles."

"Thank you, Mrs. Phillips…"

"And this must be Audrey…"

The school was designed so that the main hall ran north-south, and the trio kept walking even as the two adult women held a conversation, as if Audrey wasn't even there. The girl's eyes focused intently on the south end of the hall, where a stairway ran to the second floor, and a stained glass window told the visual story of St. Francis de Asis.

Finally, Mrs. Phillips bent at the waist and pointed Audrey toward a classroom toward the end of the hall. A dapper young teacher stood outside, directing some of the straggling children toward their proper destinations. Howard Stonewall was strawberry-haired and bespectacled, a youthful thirty-six year old in an argyle sweater vest and bow tie.

Mrs. Phillips spoke softly to Audrey. "And that is Mr. Stonewall's classroom. He's expecting you."

Audrey looked up at her mother, unconvinced.

Liz gave her a reassuring smile. "You go ahead, honey. I'll be back at 3:15 to get you." She hugged her unsure daughter and patted her on her way.

As Audrey crossed the hall, she glanced toward the south landing to see a nun in the familiar black and white habit leading a young boy by the arm toward the stairwell to the second floor. As if aware of Audrey's gaze, the nun suddenly turned her head, giving the young girl a baleful glare without ceasing her stride. She disappeared up the stairs and out of sight, the boy in tow.

"You must be Audrey."

Surprised, Audrey looked up to see Mr. Stonewall smiling at her. She nodded awkwardly.

"Please join us," the teacher said softly, directing her toward the classroom.

She cast one more glance at the now empty landing, where the sun streamed through the window in multicolored bands of light. As Audrey left the hall, Mr. Stonewall happened to notice Liz standing with Mrs. Phillips and offered a nod of greeting before heading in as the last bell rang.

Liz watched her daughter disappear into the classroom and returned her attention to Faye Phillips. "I'm so glad you were able to fit her in. It was a last minute thing, and I really hate having to pull her out of her old school, but—"

Faye's expression was sympathy personified. "I understand, Mrs. Charles. I do."

The two women turned and began ambling toward the north entrance.

Liz let her next words slip out before fully vetting their meaning. "We needed a change."

Ah yes. Hello, Awkward Pause, my old friend.

They were perhaps twenty yards from the school entrance when Faye stopped, and pulled Liz aside. "I'm not trying to pry...but...would you like me to set up a meeting for Audrey with the school counselor?"

Liz cleared her throat, flustered at the suggestion. "Uh, we're still talking through some stuff at home. I was going to go meet the pastor, introduce myself."

That seemed to do the trick. Faye's mask of concern melted into a radiant smile. "Oh, terrific! You'll like Father Felix. He's wonderful."

Liz returned the smile, but it was robotic, by-the-numbers. "But outside of the Church, I haven't set anything up yet. I want to get the lay of the land."

Faye's smile faded, and it was back to business. "Well I'm happy to give you some referrals if you'd like." She touched Liz's arm and their gaze lingered momentarily. "And don't worry about Audrey—we'll take good care of her, Mrs. Charles."

Liz sighed, gathering her bag strap higher on her shoulder. "Thanks."

The two women shook hands and Liz departed through the double doors, anxious to return home. The house wasn't going to unpack and organize itself. *More's the pity,* thought Liz, indulging a quick fantasy of herself as Samantha Stevens in *Bewitched.* White capri housewife pants and a cute blond bouffant. 1970s suburbia made real. A wiggle of her nose with a tinkling bell sound effect and clothes would magically leap from boxes, fold themselves in midair, and land in neat stacks in the dresser drawers.

She chuckled wistfully, finding her car along the street and thumbing the key fob to unlock the door. Casting a quick glance up at the old brick building, she caught the dour face of a nun in black and white vestments, staring down from one of the second story windows.

A crow cawed at her from the bough of a nearby cedar, and Liz instinctively looked in its direction. When she returned her gaze to the window, the nun was gone.

CHAPTER 4

Liz unlocked the front door and entered the new house, pausing for a moment in the doorway. It felt cavernous, far too large for a single adult and preteen child. She felt the emptiness of it, despite the stacks of boxes. The weight of loneliness.

Boxes. Right.

Closing the door behind her, she shed her purse and keys on the dining room table and took in her world.

But before I can get to the boxes, I'd better fuel up.

A new bottle of rosé awaited her in the fridge. Although late in the season to be drinking such a summer wine, it was the perfect solution to the problem at hand, namely what to self-medicate with. It was either some pink wine, or one of a selection of pills, and if she chose the latter, there was no guarantee she'd be awake when it was time to pick up Audrey at the end of the school day. With the pop of the cork and a gurgle into the glass, she was off to the races.

Room by room she went, her own well-practiced methodology almost instinctual. Jase had served three long tours in Afghanistan and one abbreviated mission in Somalia, and Liz had kept and moved houses on and off-base, from apartments to town-homes to duplexes. Their last place in San Diego was a McMansion in Breanna Estates, Oceanside, close enough to Camp Pendleton for Jase to commute. And she'd grown up a military brat. Her father, a Marine Colonel, had moved his family twice a year with a series of desk assignments. She was used to the process, and had it down to a science.

She did the living room first, ripping open boxes and shoving books onto bookshelves, putting sentimental knick-knacks into the built-in Tudor alcoves. Then the kitchen, squaring away pots, pans and utensils. It was the perfect amount of cabinet and drawer space. Of course it was. Liz had a knack for filling storage in a house just by looking at a photo.

Then she poured another glass of rosé and tackled Audrey's room. The wardrobe boxes fell like Napoleonic soldiers. Hangers found the closet rod. Folded clothes found dresser drawers. The graphic novels and comics Audrey and Jase used to read together found the bottom of her bookcase. Plush animals were placed in a fluffy orgy at the head of the bed. She strung fairy lights across the wall, and called it good. Audrey could figure out where to hang her artwork and posters later.

By noon, Liz was passed out asleep on the living room sofa, empty rosé bottle on the coffee table next to an equally-empty glass. By 3, she was rousting herself, cursing silently to the empty home, and finding her keys to go pick up Audrey from school. By 5, she was the happy homemaker again—or a reasonable facsimile thereof—flitting from the kitchen to the dining room to check on Audrey's homework.

At 5:15, Sandra appeared at the front door, bottle of Scarlet Grove Washington Pinot Noir tucked under her arm. Evening light from the street poured into the house as Liz opened the door to her realtor.

"Sandra! Come in!"

The vivacious blond was all smiles. "Hi hi! Happy housewarming!"

Liz paused, initially taken aback. "Is that—? First the basket, now wine?"

Sandra handed over the bottle and stepped into the living room, looking around in wonder at Liz's handiwork. Not a box was left in the living room, full, empty, or otherwise. Pictures and framed art pieces were hung. An oriental rug claimed the middle of the space, while a sofa and two matching arm chairs created the perfect conversation zone. The fireplace was ablaze in a flickering orange glow, and it looked as though Liz and Audrey had always lived there.

"College friend notwithstanding, I want my clients to feel welcome, and just wanted to check in," Sandra offered, impressed at the organization and level of cleanliness.

"Well, come in," Liz beckoned, taking the wine to the kitchen. "I'm just making dinner." She returned to her pots on the stove while Sandra ended up in the dining room, hovering just over Audrey's left shoulder.

"It sure smells delicious!" At first, she didn't notice that the eleven-year-old girl sat sketching on a pad of art paper, in a comic book style. "Honestly, most of my clients order takeout the whole first week in a new house.

I'm impressed you got your kitchen unpacked in one day!"

The reply from the kitchen was succinct. "Used to moving."

"Right." Glancing over, Sandra saw that Audrey was drawing, and it was remarkably good for a girl so young. "Wow, Audrey, you're quite the artist..." She quickly caught herself, however, realizing *what* Audrey was drawing, and a look of awkward shock flashed across her face.

On the paper, Audrey had rendered a pile of burning corpses among a carpet of stones and rubble, and her father, in uniform, carrying a small child to safety. The "comic book" Audrey watched from atop a hill in the background, holding hands with a boy in a suit and tie. Considering the age of the artist, the quality was remarkably good. The subject matter, on the other hand...

"It's about my dad," Audrey chimed without drama or irony.

Sandra swallowed dryly.

Liz poked her head out of the kitchen, drying her hands on a dish towel. "Do you want to stay for dinner?"

Taking Liz aside in the kitchen doorway, Sandra muttered closely to her with parental concern. "You know what? Thank you, but I don't want to intrude." She gave a subtle nod toward Audrey at the table. "I think Audrey needs her mama tonight."

Liz looked surprised. "Wha—? You sure you won't stay?"

"I'm sure. But I'll call you tomorrow and check in, okay?" The blond realtor's ebullience returned. She could take the edge off most situations with her bubbly smile.

Liz, still unsure of what had just happened, started to follow Sandra to the door, her face furrowed like a broken plate. "Yeah. Sure."

Sandra batted artificial eyelashes. "I'll let myself out—enjoy the wine. Lovely to see you both. Buh-bye!"

A human tornado smelling of lilac and shea butter, Sandra exited the house, and Liz looked after her for a frustrated moment. *What on Earth—?*

"My comic scared her."

Liz moved casually to look over Audrey's shoulder. Taking in the graphic bloodbath in black ink and colored pencil, she pulled up a chair next to her daughter at the table. "Oh Audrey, honey."

Audrey's tone was patronizing. "Mr. Stonewall says we should draw what we feel inside, and that can help when we're sad."

"Well that's very wise of Mr. Stonewall," Liz affirmed, her heart breaking for her child. "I'm just...you're so young to be going through this."

Audrey remembered a platitude she once heard an adult say. "We still have each other, right?"

"Yes we do, sweetie," Liz smiled, hugging Audrey to her and looking at the drawing in more detail. She pointed at the little girl figure in the drawing, then at the boy.

"Is this you?"

Audrey nodded.

"And who's this?"

"Caleb Douglas." Audrey fell suddenly somber.

"Who's that? Someone from school?"

"Yeah. He's new too. Nobody talks to him either."

"Well that's so wonderful of you to be his friend."

Audrey frowned. "He's nice. But his clothes are dirty. I think his family might be poor."

Liz rose from the chair and returned to the kitchen to tend her cooking. "Well I'm still very proud of you for taking him under your wing, when you're the new kid too."

Audrey continued coloring, Liz facing away for a moment to tend her pots. When she turned back to tell her daughter to clean up, Audrey was no longer sitting at the table.

Liz took a step into the dining room and startled as she caught Audrey out of the corner of her eye. Her daughter stood, frozen in place, at the picture window in the living room, staring out into the front yard and the rural street beyond. Her focus was intense. Something clearly had seized her attention.

Liz did her best to push past the creeping gloom. "Honey?"

"How long 'til dinner?" Audrey asked, her voice monotone.

"About five minutes. Go get washed up?"

"Okay..."

As Liz turned back toward the kitchen, Audrey stepped away from the picture window to head to the bathroom. As she broke away, her reflection lingered momentarily in the glass pane before disappearing.

CHAPTER 5

A distant thunder clap, or an improvised explosive device...

Captain Charles carried the Afghan child, striding in slow motion in front of a billowing cloud of fire, smoke and death. In the next moment, he was an eternity away, torn to pieces on the pile of rubble and broken pallets. Liz watched as her mind's movie camera zoomed in on Jase's charred and blistered face. Two red, hemorrhaged eyes snapped open.

Once again, Liz woke with a start, gasping for air—labored breathing that immediately deteriorated into sobs. It made no sense. She knew when Jase died, he'd been missing an eye. Why now was she seeing two? And what was with the gut-wrenching sense of urgency? It had to be her imagination again, filling in the gaps. Her fucking imagination. She was furious. It needed to be tamed.

Again she fumbled for the prescription bottle in her bedside drawer, swallowing two capsules and washing them down with a gulp from her wine glass. This time she left the drawer open and rolled into the fetal position, hugging a spare pillow to her chest.

The bedside clock read 3:17 a.m.

◌

Day two.

Liz poured hot water from a boiling tea kettle into a small French press, where it mixed with coffee grounds and swelled up in the carafe. In a process that took several minutes, she was only really aware of brief snippets, flying on autopilot. She plunged the press down. Poured the coffee in to a mug. Slammed the hot beverage back.

Wearing workout clothes and a windbreaker, she put in her own earbuds and cranked up some her workout playlist, a healthy combination of '80s and '90s alternative. Then she tied a pair of running shoes and took off like a rocket into the rural streets outside.

Tuesday.

Liz ran, as steeped in memories as the coffee grounds had been in the French press...

That time, in our first apartment, when we slow-danced barefoot on the hardwood floors.

When Audrey was four, and you taught her chess, because why not? You insisted that four wasn't too early to learn chess. And I watched that four-year-old absolutely crush you after all of three lessons.

The volleyball and cookouts on Coronado Beach.

All those countless lazy weekend mornings, we lay in bed after making love, and you would tell me the stupidest dad jokes imaginable. Especially the one about the broccoli.

I miss those times.

I miss us.

Damnit, Jason, I miss you.

It was your last deployment! Why did it have to be when you were four weeks short?

Why?

Jesus, I could kill you for dying on me.

As she sprinted into the brisk morning air, Liz was comforted by the fact that her red-rimmed, swollen eyes and streaming tears would seem like simple tree allergies.

The rest of the afternoon was the same autopilot and a cascade of snippets, just like the morning had been. She stood in her bedroom, facing a stack of moving boxes with a glass of wine in one hand. She pulled packing tape off a moving box. Pulled open box flaps. Gulped from the wine glass. Opened another box. Pried open more flaps. Gulped more wine.

Suddenly she found herself in the bedroom with several open boxes around the room. Like the egg nursery in *Aliens*, each one held a potential face-hugger, ready to implant another painful memory. Some had Jase's old uniform pieces. Others contained random family items. Liz reached into the box in front of her and produced a small stack of photos.

Sorting through the photos, she determined most to be of Jase and the family, candids from younger, happier days. She stopped on a photo of the two of them together at a Marine Corps formal ball. Then, looking past the photos, she spied something else in the box. Digging deeply, she retrieved a set of dog tags stamped with:

CHARLES

JASON A. O POS

555-77-0541

USMC L

CATHOLIC

Liz clutched the formal photo and dog tags to her chest as she climbed onto the bed and curled up like a hedgehog, sobbing silently.

CHAPTER 6

The black Jeep pulled up to the curb in front of the school, and Liz shut off the engine. She looked hastily put together, as if she only recently woke up from her nap, which, of course, was the case. Through the passenger side window, she could see Audrey playing with a young boy about her age who was wearing a threadbare blue sweater, tie and slacks. It must have been her new friend, Caleb Douglas. The two children kicked a soccer ball back and forth in a blacktop area designated for four-square. A few other school kids played in the vicinity while awaiting their parents and assorted after-school rides. Howard Stonewall looked on from atop the stairs outside the rear exit, the recess monitor king surveying his domain.

As Liz exited the car to enter the playground blacktop, she noticed the soccer ball go bouncing down a set of concrete steps and through an exterior basement door. Without a word, Caleb dashed down after it into the dark.

Liz approached, watching as Audrey stood by the open door at the top of the concrete stairwell, yelling down into the basement.

"Caleb? Throw it back up here!"

"Audrey, honey, I'm here," Liz announced, arriving with a smile.

Audrey stared into the dark stairwell to the basement. "Throw it back!"

"Is that Caleb you're playing with?"

"He's not coming up."

"Well honey, he's probably looking for the ball. I'll go get him." Producing a mobile phone from her jacket and thumbing the flashlight app, Liz descended into the basement.

From across the playground, Mr. Stonewall cast an anxious look and began to cross the blacktop toward Audrey, standing perfectly still at the top of the stairwell.

The school basement was a typical industrial space from the turn of the 1900s: a dimly-lit storage area with wooden shelves around the perimeter, stacks of scrap lumber and debris, and plenty of soot and cement dust. An ancient boiler sat in the rear corner. Liz arrived at the bottom of the basement stairs, taking shallow breaths to avoid the dust and the smell. It was more than simply musty—far more. It smelled like the decay of formerly living things. She knew it was a cliché, but it smelled like death.

Aiming the LED flashlight beam into the darkness, she caught a glimpse of a small shadow moving in the dark, and heard the shuffle of small feet.

"Caleb?"

She looked curiously at the boiler, conflicted on whether to probe into the dark basement.

"Caleb? You okay?"

A soft tapping erupted at her feet as the soccer ball bounced out of the shadows, rolling to a stop at her feet. She bent down to pick it up, standing to find herself facing a giant of a man.

She startled, uttering a tiny yelp of surprise.

He towered over her, a pale hulk in filthy coveralls which might have been a dark blue once upon a time. Enormous, calloused hands held fingers like bratwursts, curled as if ready to strangle a neck. The fingernails that weren't chewed or torn away were stained yellow with nicotine, fungus, or industrial chemicals. Savage eyes stared out from under a heavy brow. His dark hair was matted down with sweat and grease and his lips sported the occasional vertical scar.

Some janitor, she thought. *How does he not scare the children every day?*

Liz held the soccer ball in front of her like the worst shield ever. "Oh! I was just retrieving this...have you seen a boy down here?"

The custodian stared intently, and Liz felt panic rising in her throat. The thick fingers flexed, and a bead of sweat rolled down one blackened cheek.

"I'd better go..." With the ball between her and the giant janitor, Liz inched her way toward the steps leading up to the playground. She arrived at the top of the stairwell to find Audrey standing next to the nun from the school hallway. The severe-looking woman was perhaps in her fifties, with deep furrows in her face at all the usual stress points, and she was whispering into Audrey's ear. Seeing Liz approach, she bared yellow teeth and disappeared into a small group of children near the jungle gym.

Audrey stood absolutely still. She appeared transfixed, almost hypnotized. Like she had at the living room window the previous night.

"I found it, sweetie," Liz announced, showing her daughter the soccer ball in question.

"Sister Beatrice said you shouldn't go down there," came Audrey's raspy reply.

"Who?"

"She said it isn't safe down there."

Mr. Stonewall arrived to find Liz unnerved. "Mrs. Charles?"

Liz dropped the ball and took Audrey by the hand. It was time to go. As she urged the young girl toward the Jeep next to the blacktop, she threw a pointed admonishment to Howard Stonewall. "You might wanna check to make sure Caleb is okay." Then, to Audrey: "We should get home. Come on, honey."

Liz pulled Audrey along as Mr. Stonewall gestured for her attention.

"I'm sorry? Mrs. Charles, I'm hoping that we can set up a time to meet—"

"Thank you, Mr. Stonewall, I'll come see you soon." Liz and Audrey crossed behind the monkey bars and walked quickly toward the car.

Mr. Stonewall stood at the top of the basement steps, bewildered. "I have some time after class on Friday…"

"Sounds great," Liz replied, not looking back.

From a second story classroom window, Faye Phillips watched the scene on the playground, watched as Liz put Audrey in the car, watched Mr. Stonewall stoop to pick up the abandoned soccer ball.

He stood alone by the stairwell to the boiler room door, which was closed. Frowning, he shuffled down the first few steps to check it. He tested the handle, seeing that it was indeed locked. The door didn't budge.

Liz got into the Jeep and shut the car door. As she turned on the ignition, she glanced out the passenger window at the playground. Mr. Stonewall stared back at her briefly, then turned to walk away. She angled back toward the steering wheel, and something caught her eye out the driver's side window.

Sister Beatrice stood glaring at Liz, leaning over not two feet from the car.

Liz jumped, breathing hard.

The nun glared through judging eyes, putting her index finger to her lips as if admonishing Liz to be quiet.

Heart hammering in her chest, Liz put the Jeep in gear and peeled away.

CHAPTER 7

A half-empty pizza box sat in the middle of the dining table, along with an empty bottle of wine, and another on its way to empty. Liz and Sandra sat next to plates smeared with the grease and tomato sauce of the evening's culinary conquest, Liz with her crusts stacked neatly to one side. Each woman held the stem of a wine glass with a big pour of red. The atmosphere was close, warm, and truthful—if a bit on the tipsy side.

"How very strange," Sandra offered, fully in the thrall of the Cabernet.

Liz rolled her eyes in solidarity, refreshing her glass from the rapidly depleting bottle. "I couldn't believe it. One of their students was missing in the basement, and she's berating Audrey for me going down there."

"And you never found him?"

Liz shook her head *no*. "I assumed they found him after we left. Audrey's teacher was right there and this Sister Beatrice was aware of the whole situation."

Sandra's blue eyes suddenly took on a mischievous glint. "Howard Stonewall is Audrey's teacher, yes?"

Liz swallowed from her glass, nodding. "You know him?"

"I sold him his house. He's very smart..." Sandra said, adding, "and very single."

Liz smiled, amused by Sandra's drunken machinations. "He's very young."

"Nothing wrong with that," Sandra winked.

Liz leveled a look of theatrical surprise at her blond college friend. "Sandra. I'm shocked."

"I didn't think anything could shock a Catholic girl."

"It's true," Liz giggled, and the two shared a laugh, each remembering the exploits of younger days.

When the laughter had softened to chuckles, and each taken another sip of wine, Sandra looked at her friend, trying to find Liz's eyes through the haze of their mutual inebriation.

"How you doing, really?"

Liz's heart sank like a stone, taking her mood and her buzz with it. "I don't know. What do you want me to say?"

Sandra wiped back a tear that threatened to streak her mascara. "I wish I'd known him. Jason."

"Yeah," Liz sighed, adding with a wink, "kinda glad you didn't, just the same."

Sandra feigned offense at the implication that she would have stolen Jase like any other college boyfriend, but the wine made her belly warm and a broad smile played across her face. "Oh, hey!" she interjected. "Have you talked to Father Felix yet?"

Liz stalled. "Uh, yeah. It's on the agenda."

"You should. He's really a great listener."

Audrey appeared at the bottom of the stairs, face washed and clad in an oversize My Chemical Romance concert shirt and pajama pants.

Both women straightened, trying to act a little less drunk.

Sandra beamed. "Ah, there she is!"

"All set?" Liz asked.

Audrey nodded. "Ready."

Sandra glanced at her bare wrist. "Is it that time already?"

"Relax," Liz assured her. "Finish your wine. I just need to check homework, and I'll be back down."

Sandra was already killing the last red in the bottle. "Twist my arm."

Liz tilted her head and nodded toward Sandra. Audrey rolled her eyes and smiled. She padded across the hardwood floors to Sandra and embraced her in a big hug.

"Good night, Sandra."

"Oh, good night, dear."

Audrey inhaled the scent of lilac bodywash and cocoa butter, then released the realtor and took her mother's hand as Liz rose from the table and led her back to the stairs.

"Okay, you. Let's go."

"Have you seen Dad's dog tags?" Audrey asked.

They climbed the oak staircase, bare feet treading almost silently.

"Yes, as a matter of fact," Liz answered, producing the metal tags from the back pocket of her jeans. "I found them in one of the boxes yesterday."

Audrey's bedroom was warmly decorated with preteen girl sensibilities. A few stuffed animals and plush toys competed with art supplies and Lego creations for table and floor space. She was in that "tween" transition, between kids' toys and more grown-up pursuits. A framed family photo sat on her bedside table and a crucifix hung on her wall. The stringed lights lent a fairy tale ambiance to the room, illuminating walls lined with music posters and comic book art. A new promotional poster from *Torchlight Lullaby* was proudly displayed above the head of Audrey's bed, a prize from Ryan Fisher's visit to Comics-N-Stuff in Chula Vista earlier that spring.

Audrey climbed into bed as Liz handed the dog tags to her and began to flip through her school binder, sorting through various homework assignments.

"Mom?"

"Hmm?"

"Dad... he's really dead, right?"

Liz looked shocked that such a question could come out of her daughter's mouth. "I would never joke about that. And we certainly wouldn't have moved away."

"So why can I hear him sometimes?"

Liz sat on the edge of Audrey's bed, patting her leg under the covers as Audrey fidgeted with the dog tags. "Well, some people believe our loved ones can talk to us from heaven."

"You think dad's in heaven?"

"I'm sure he is, sweetie. Your father was a good person."

The young girl pondered for a moment, gazing at the family portrait and the tags before looking back at her mom. "He talks to me."

Liz smiled, tears starting to well up as she let Audrey keep going.

"Like he's with me in the same room."

"What does he tell you?"

"He tells me he loves us."

A tearful laugh erupted from Liz. She covers her mouth to hide the reaction, reaching down to hold Audrey's hand.

"He tells me he's sad we moved away..."

Liz sighed, pulling her hands into her own lap. "Oh, honey..."

Audrey looked at her mother earnestly. "And he told me not to talk to the bad man anymore."

Liz startled. "What? Who?"

"The janitor in the school basement. The one who took our soccer ball."

"When, um... when did you talk to him?" Liz queried, trying desperately to keep her cool.

"In the hallway yesterday. He doesn't like kids very much. Sister Beatrice says he's harmless, but I think there's something wrong with him."

Liz paused, silently terrified at the revelation. "Well you listen to your dad. You stay away from that basement and away from the janitor. And from that...Sister Beatrice too, for that matter."

"Okay."

Liz relaxed, sliding next to Audrey on her mattress. "Good. I love you."

"I love you too, Mom." Audrey grabbed her mother tightly, a quizzical look appearing as Liz stood to leave the room. "What about our prayer?"

Liz winced. She shouldn't have forgotten. It was normal bedtime routine. "Right. Sorry."

As her mother sank to her knees next to the bed, Audrey closed her eyes and began to recite the familiar Hail Mary prayer. Liz joined in during the second line.

Hail Mary, full of grace.

Our Lord is with thee.

Blessed art thou among women,

and blessed is the fruit of thy womb, Jesus.

Holy Mary, Mother of God,

pray for us sinners,

now and at the hour of our death.

Amen.

Liz took Audrey's hands in her own and led the personalized section of the bedtime prayer. "Heavenly Father, we thank you for the day we had and for a restful night to come. And we pray for..." She trailed off as a cue for Audrey to insert the names of those she wanted to add to the celestial guest list.

"My dad," said Audrey.

"Your dad."

"Grandma and Grandpa."

"Good, and who else?"

"And..." Audrey thought for a moment, then added, "Mr. Stonewall. He's nice."

Then it was Liz's turn to make some suggestions. "And Sandra, who got us this nice home and brought us dinner tonight?"

"Yes, and Sandra."

Each made the sign of the cross, repeating the benediction in unison: "In the name of the Father, and of the Son, and of the Holy Spirit, Amen."

Bedtime holy rites satisfied, Liz leaned forward to kiss Audrey on the forehead. "Good night, sweetie."

"Good night, Mom."

Liz smiled, tucking her daughter into bed and turning off the light switch by the dresser, which doused the fairy string and left the room illuminated by a small color-cycling night light in the corner. She paused in the open doorway. "Open or closed?"

Audrey peeked from her soft vantage, face partially buried in a stuffed panda and a thick duvet. "Closed is fine."

Liz ducked out of the bedroom, quietly shutting the door.

"Goodnight, Dad," Audrey whispered to the darkened space around her.

"Goodnight, Dumpling," the darkness replied.

CHAPTER 8

Day three.

Wednesday was as drab and gray as any other Wednesday in Slaughter County. Audrey had been assigned a book report, and had chosen a history of the local area, because she was a colossal nerd like her father. And one of the first things she'd learned from the book was that the place was originally named for a young 19th century Army officer called Slaughter.

West Point graduate Captain William Alloway Slaughter and his wife, Mary, were part of the ever-increasing population of white fortune seekers pouring into the Oregon and Washington territories in the 1850s. Blessed by the Unites States government, they came armed with treaties and guns, and usually ended up relying on the latter—even if the former were successful.

In a conflict with the local Nisqually Indians, Captain Slaughter was killed by a musket ball in the heart, ending life as his own namesake. The county would later be rechartered as Kitsap, after a Suquamish war chief. But Audrey loved the ring of "Slaughter County". It felt more accurate, somehow, given the gloom and the ever-present stench of moss and dead fish at low-tide.

School kids ran to and fro, exiting the facility to the arms of waiting parents. Liz knew Audrey was writing an initial outline for her report, and would likely still be in Mr. Stonewall's classroom. As she made her way down the now spartan and quiet hallway, Faye Phillips emerged from the side office door to intercept her.

"Mrs. Charles?"

Liz smiled, but it was a cool, forced affair. "Hello, Mrs. Phillips."

"May I have a quick word?" the principal asked, gesturing toward an old church pew now functioning as a hallway bench.

The two women sat.

"I was wondering...I heard from Mr. Stonewall yesterday about the incident at the basement..."

"Oh, there really wasn't an incident," Liz protested, minimizing the episode.

Mrs. Phillips was undaunted. "It's just that we keep the exterior basement door locked during school hours for safety reasons, and we just can't allow parents to go exploring down there unescorted—"

Liz held up a hand to stop her. "Hold on, let's get this straight. I was *not* 'exploring'. Audrey's soccer ball went down the stairs and Caleb wasn't bringing it up, so I went to fetch it."

"But that's impossible, since the door is always—"

Liz stood, thoroughly done with the conversation. "Look. Faye, the door was wide open. I'm really not interested in a lecture right now. If you have a problem with people going into the basement, maybe talk to that walking mountain of a janitor and make sure it stays locked when the kids are playing."

Audrey appeared from the classroom at the end of the hall, running to meet her mother, who she grabbed in a casual side hug. "Hey Mom."

Mr. Stonewall waved to the trio from his classroom doorway, disappearing back inside.

At the end of the hall, Sister Beatrice strolled down the last few oak stairs and continued silently down a side corridor.

Liz shivered. "So if that's all, we really need to be going."

Mrs. Phillips stood as Liz and Audrey started toward the main doors. "But I'm still not clear on how—"

"Like I said," Liz interrupted, offering her final word on the subject, "if you want answers, talk to the janitor. Come on, honey."

Liz and Audrey bustled down the hall, heading for the front doors and the Jeep outside.

Faye stared after them, dumbfounded.

⟠

Liz and Audrey exited the Jeep in front of the small Catholic church, pulling their jackets closer against the crisp autumn air. The sanctuary, modest by historical standards, was awash in beams of vividly-colored daylight through stained glass. The pews sat almost completely empty, save for a few random parishioners, praying by themselves.

As the two quietly entered through the narthex into the nave, years of traditional programming took over. Dipping an index finger into the open bowl of holy water near the exit, they crossed themselves. Audrey went forward to an alcove full of small white candles, some lit, some not. Plucking an unlit one from the box on the canted wooden shelf, she ignited the wick from another candle and placed it in a holder. Making the sign of the cross again, she knelt in front of the alcove in a silent prayer for her father's soul.

Liz genuflected toward the effigy of the Holy Mother at the front of the transept, and slid stealthily into one of the unoccupied rear pews.

From a side office, someone noticed Audrey's arrival and the candle lighting. He wore the black regulation clothing of a priest engaged in his day-to-day non-ceremonial duties: the matching chinos, button-down shirt with white clerical collar, and blazer of a modern man of the cloth. He was ginger-complected, his dark red hair cropped short and beginning to thin on top. Eyes of crystal blue probed from beneath a heavy brow, seeming to drink everything in and file the information away for later. The man appeared somewhere between thirty-five and sixty, depending on proximity and lighting. His facial skin was pulled taut across pronounced cheekbones and a gaunt, chiseled jaw, appearing craggy and scarred over much of its surface—from acne, burns, weather exposure, or some combination thereof. His mouth was a straight line, brow furrowed to a permanently troubled arch over a hawk nose. There was a profound darkness to the man, held at bay behind that weathered face and those all-seeing eyes.

Slipping from the office down the left aisle, the priest crept to the pew where Liz sat and slid in a few feet away from her without making a sound.

"Took you long enough." His whispered voice carried a mild New York accent, and was almost sinister in the sanctuary's gloom.

Liz turned, stunned at the sudden, strange comment. "I'm sorry?"

"I understand. It's a long drive up from Pendleton, you had to get unpacked." The thin lips parted in a wry smile, revealing uneven teeth.

Liz paused, shocked at the priest's unusual manner. "Yes...how...?"

"We've been expecting you, Mrs. Charles."

"Wait...are you...?"

"Felix Connelly. I'm the pastor of St. Francis. Welcome to our community." He offered Liz his hand and she shook it warmly.

"Thank you. I...I'm not used to..."

"I'm not a stickler for formality, Mrs. Charles," he said softly.

"Well in that case, you can call me Liz."

"All right, Liz. Is there anything we can do to help you settle in?"

Liz froze in response. She hadn't prepared for any of this. Her mind sorted through a thousand different responses. Finally, she relaxed, realizing this was why she remained with the Church. It took care of its community. "Actually, there is one thing..."

"Fire away."

"My husband...Jason...he was...killed in action in Afghanistan..."

Felix nodded in understanding. "Father Martin called to tell me, which is how I knew to expect you. I'm very sorry for your family's loss."

Liz took a deep, uncomfortable breath. Although gratified to hear her old priest in San Diego had called ahead, she was used to doing this in a closed confessional, not in an open pew. Still, the closest other person was several benches in front of her, lost in an open Bible. If she kept her voice to a whisper...

"Thanks. Okay, so I've uprooted my daughter and moved a thousand miles away. I feel like I've forsaken my family, and I might be causing emotional harm to my child."

"Do you have a phone?" mused the priest.

"What? Yes. Of course."

"Then you haven't forsaken your family. Do you love your daughter?

"Of course. Why would that even—?"

"Does she know?"

"Yes. I tell her every day."

"And you keep her best interest in mind?"

"Of course."

"Children are resilient, Liz. You're likely not causing any permanent damage."

"I've been having dreams...nightmares, really."

Felix tilted his head toward Liz, while he remained focused on the altar at the front of the sanctuary. "These things are quite common among the bereaved," he said with authority.

"They are?"

"It's a way for our minds to make sense of a situation which will never make sense."

Liz took the information in, and Father Felix continued.

"Does he say anything in the dreams?"

"It's like he tries, but I can never hear him —it's just really chaotic and it's like I'm there with him in the war zone. You're sure it's normal?

"Absolutely normal. We can talk more at length tomorrow morning if you like. I have eleven o'clock free. Stop by the church office."

"Okay. Sure. Thank you, Father..." Liz smiled, as if finding an ally for the first time.

Felix rose silently from the pew, turning to Liz and offering a blessing. "I know this wasn't a formal confession, but just to be safe..." He traced a cross in the air, reciting the Latin: "*Ego te absolvo. In nomine Patris, et Filii, et Spiritus Sancti. Amen.*"

I absolve you.

In the name of the Father, and the Son, and the Holy Spirit.

Liz crossed herself again in response. "Amen." Sliding out of the pew, she retrieved Audrey from the alcove and they exited the church together.

Felix watched them leave, glaring like a gargoyle in the center of the aisle.

CHAPTER 9

The red numbers of the bedside alarm clock read 3:16 a.m. Liz Charles' sleeping form rose and fell with the breathing of deep REM sleep.

She could see him.

The quality was better now, not grainy or abstract. Jason Charles carried the Afghan child across the piles of singed bricks and debris, the sirens of emergency vehicles wailing in the distance—converging with the cries of the wounded and bereaved.

She watched his steps, crying out in her head to warn him of the second explosive device.

Please Jase, don't step there. Anywhere else. Please just not there. Don't step—

The second explosion rocketed through Liz's dreaming brain, a deafening sound and furious blast of heat. Her body tensed as if she were there. The light and smoke were blinding. She coughed imaginary dust and debris away. The haze gradually cleared as Liz pushed forward with the camera of her mind, zooming in on the bloody, dismembered body of her husband. Pieces missing. Guts strewn across the rubble around his sundered torso. And then those hemorrhaged eyes popped open, full of pain, full of fear.

But also full of warning.

The bloody lips peeled back on stark white teeth, as his mouth tried to phrase a word.

Help them.

It was his voice, crystal clear in her head. It was choked and wet with aspirated blood, but it was Jase.

Help them.

The clock read 3:17 a.m.

Liz woke with her usual start, but her room was far from its normal state of nighttime quiet. She could hear hushed voices talking around her, their words subtle and indistinguishable, like garbled voices on a radio. She could feel someone in the room with her, though the falloff from the streetlamp outside revealed nothing in the shadows.

Frowning, she hoisted herself upright and turned on the bedside lamp. She padded barefoot to the master bathroom, clad in a pair of Jase's boxer shorts and an olive drab USMC t-shirt. The voices followed, every creaky footstep in the house magnified into a hideous finger scratching at the wall. She turned on the tap and splashed a few handfuls of cool water on her face, patting dry as she—

What was that in the mirror?

That face, those watchful eyes...

"Jason?" Liz gasped, spinning around to see...nothing.

Suddenly, wafting in over the indistinct, disembodied voices from the dark, what sounded like a shushing noise.

Scurrying to the bathroom window overlooking the back yard, Liz peered out to where a low fence backed up to a green belt behind the house. There stood a stark figure in the gray glow of the moonlight. A familiar silhouette.

Sister Beatrice watched the house with a burning intensity.

"—the hell?" Furious, Liz marched from the bathroom, plucking her robe from the foot of the bed and shrugging into it as she headed for the stairs. The voices grew distant and soft as her anger focused, but they did not disappear completely. She cleared the staircase and flung open the kitchen door to the back patio, half-expecting the sinister nun to have departed already.

But she remained, clad in the black habit of her order, a dark shroud on a living body.

Liz slammed the back door shut and stalked toward the glaring figure of Sister Beatrice.

"Look, Sister! You have no right to show up at my home in the middle of the night—"

The nun held a finger to her lips. *"Shhhh. Secrets must be kept."*

What secrets? Liz thought. *What is she talking about?*

"Is this about the basement?" Liz moved forward, spoiling to return some of the hurt she was feeling. The voices increased in volume, still indistinct, but unnerving in their intensity.

She felt something—a hand on her shoulder. "Help them, Liz."

Jason?

Hearing her husband's voice, Liz whirled around to see—

—nothing on the back patio.

She turned again back to where Sister Beatrice—

—was gone.

The voices bled away into the shadows. Into silence.

Liz stood alone in the back yard, terrified. Conflicted. There was a nun from the school telling her to keep secrets, and her dead husband pleading for her to help persons unknown from beyond the grave.

Unless this had all been a product of her self-medication cocktail of red wine and Ambien?

No, she decided. *No, that fucking nun was real. Standing in my back yard. Telling me to keep the basement a secret. Or whatever she was on about.*

She blinked wide eyes as she tried to gather her wits, knowing such an effort would be ultimately futile tonight.

CR

Thursday.
Day four.

Liz strode with purpose through the empty school hallway, the children already ensconced in their classrooms. She looked haggard. Her brow furrowed and jaw set, she breezed past the front desk receptionist and into Faye Phillips' office.

Faye looked up from her desk, surprised at the interruption. "Mrs. Charles, did we—?"

"Cut the shit, Faye," Liz spat, letting her anger swell as she paced the small office. "I'm not in the mood this morning. I want to know what right you think you have to send school personnel to my home at O-dark-thirty to threaten me."

Mrs. Phillips gave her a concerned look. "I'm sure I don't know what you mean. When was this?"

"Last night. About 3:30 a.m."

"And who was there?"

"Sister Beatrice. The nun who scolded Audrey after I went into the school basement the other day."

Faye looked confused. "*Sister* Beatrice?"

"Don't pretend you don't know," Liz shot back. "I understand you not wanting to face liability if an accident had happened, but come on. Your janitor left the door wide open."

"That's right. I wanted to have you talk to Mr. Dobbs." Faye picked up her desk phone and punched a number. Liz could hear her voice over the intercom speakers. "Mr. Dobbs to the principal's office, please." Setting the phone back on its cradle, she gestured toward a chair. "Please sit down, Mrs. Charles. Let's discuss this."

Liz regarded Faye with suspicion, but eventually took a seat near a corner file cabinet. "Anyway, I was worried that the little boy might have been hurt. But certainly I don't need a visit from Mother Superior to scare me into good behavior. I've had enough swollen knuckles to last a lifetime."

"But Mrs. Charles...Liz..."

"What."

"You said *Sister Beatrice*."

Liz gave an exasperated sigh. "I don't know. That's what Audrey said her name was. Slender nun, mid-forties, severe face—which probably describes all of them..."

"But that's the thing," Faye explained, sadness creeping into her expression. "St. Francis School doesn't have any nuns on staff. Or priests for that matter. This school hasn't employed clergy in over fifty years."

Liz stared silently at the principal, letting the impossible information sink in. "She was on your playground yesterday. My daughter knows her by name."

Faye returned the earnest look. "I don't know what to tell you, Mrs. Charles. There are no nuns at this school."

There was a knock at the door and a middle-aged man of slight build and African extraction poked his head in. He wore work clothes and a baseball cap, which he doffed as he entered the office.

"You wanted to see me, Mrs. Phillips?"

"Yes, Mr. Dobbs. Come in. I wanted to know if you had the exterior basement door open at any time Tuesday afternoon."

"No, it's been locked from the inside since school started. I use the interior access."

Faye looked intently at Dobbs, wanting to achieve absolute clarity on the matter. "So at no point was the outside door—?"

Liz interrupted, her frustration spilling out like a bag of marbles on the floor. "Look, I don't know who this Mr. Dobbs is, but I'm talking about the *other* janitor."

"Other janitor?" Dobbs mused. He and Faye exchanged a look.

"He's huge," Liz explained. "With greasy hair and coveralls. He was *in* the basement when I went down there."

Dobbs nervously wrung the baseball cap in his hands. "Mrs. Phillips?"

Faye held up a hand, nodding. "That's all, Mr. Dobbs. Sorry for taking you from your work."

"All right." Perplexed, Dobbs exited the office.

A knowing silence descended on the room.

Finally, Liz shook her head, tears starting to swell behind her eyes. "Don't tell me."

"Mr. Dobbs is the only janitor here," Faye said softly.

Liz was defiant. "Look. I went into the basement because Caleb went after Audrey's ball and didn't come back out. I was concerned that he'd been hurt down there, so that's why I went. Did anyone even check on him? Was he ever found?"

The look on Faye's face was of sad defeat. There was only one option in her mind: Liz was clearly delusional.

"Not to my knowledge," she explained to Liz. "In fact, we don't currently have a Caleb enrolled here."

"Are you serious? Caleb... Douglas? Audrey says he's new too, so he might be under your radar."

"I know each and every one of our students, Mrs. Charles. We have no Caleb Douglas enrolled."

Liz stared for a moment with mouth agape. Then she gathered her purse and jacket and rose from the chair with all the strength and dignity she could muster. "This is ridiculous. I have to go meet with Father Felix." She paused by the office door, turning briefly to face the school administrator with red-rimmed eyes. "I didn't imagine this, Faye."

She stalked out of the office and down the hall. On her way toward the front exit, she spied a framed photo hanging on the wall. It was one of several, arrayed along the hallway walls at eye height. Photos upon photos of the former staff, going back to the turn of the twentieth century. But this one stood out, somehow. It seized her attention and would not let it go.

As she moved closer to the photo, she could make out a group portrait in black and white. Two rows of nuns and priests gazed out from their vestments of long ago.

An unmistakable Sister Beatrice glared from under her white coif.

A placard in the center proclaimed this gathering: *ST. FRANCIS SCHOOL TEACHING STAFF - 1957*

CHAPTER 10

Father Felix peered at the loose photograph from the school through the reading glasses on his nose. For the moment, a blank rectangle looked out from the array of school faculty photos in the hallway. It would eventually find its way back into the old frame.

Liz paced the modest office, full of books and documents and the occasional religious icon. It was the workspace of a man who had been there for twenty years and it showed. She stopped to look at a framed certificate—a Master's degree in psychology from NYU in the name of Felix Connelly. Impressed, she glanced above it and noted the diploma for a PhD in clinical psychology from The Catholic University of America in Washington, DC.

Father Felix squinted through the glasses on his face. "On the far right, you say?"

"Yeah."

"1957. A little before my time here."

Liz continued pacing, filling the small office with nervous energy. "According to Mrs. Phillips, St. Francis hasn't employed clergy since about that time. Audrey called her 'Sister Beatrice'."

Felix cast a concerned look across his desk at Liz. "And how is your daughter doing?"

Liz countered with a face full of pure frustration. "Oh, please don't start with me, Father. She didn't imagine the nun, or the janitor, or the boy any more than I did."

Father Felix removed his glasses and regarded Liz in an even, professorial manner. "Oh, I believe you. But hear me out. When you suffer a loss like you have, it's not uncommon...well, to experience things like dreams...or visual hallucinations. It's just the brain reacting to trauma."

Liz sighed. "I thought you were supposed to help with my grief."

"That's exactly what I'm doing," the priest said softly.

Tears finally broke through the stoic military wife facade. Liz cradled her arms together across her body. "The dreams are bad enough. I don't want to feel any more…"

"The dreams are your subconscious trying to *make* you feel," Felix explained. "When it comes to grief, there's no way out but through. Sooner or later you have to process."

Liz tried a different tack. "So what if this is the way I process? Suppose the nun is a figment of my traumatized imagination. What does it mean? And why would my daughter be hallucinating the exact same thing?"

There was a silent pause as Father Felix wrestled with the comment. "That is an *excellent* question."

As she continued pacing, Liz noticed a framed photo on a bookshelf and picked it up: a younger Felix in his mid-twenties, in Gulf-War-era Army fatigues, stood with his tank crew, smiling out at the world. The name *BLASTY BOYS* was stenciled on the tank's main gun, and the photo was labeled *BRAVO COMPANY, 1ST TIGER BDE, 3/67 2AD 'HOUNDS OF HELL'* in black Sharpie.

"You served?"

Felix had already returned his attention to the photo of Sister Beatrice and the other nuns, but he nodded in response. "Desert Storm. Tanker."

Indicating the diploma from NYU on the wall, she continued the interrogation. "From back east, huh?"

"Born and raised in New Rochelle. I was assigned here in '97."

"Why here?"

A sly smile crept across his face as he looked up at Liz. "I could say it's where they send the troublemakers...But it was really just luck of the draw." He added earnestly, "It's a good community."

Liz smiled and began to gather her things. "Can you do something for me, Father? Can you look through the school records, find out if Sister Beatrice is employed anywhere in the parish? Same with the little boy? Caleb? See if he is—or was—a student here? If you can verify that these people really exist, we can at least rule out that my daughter and I are insane."

Felix chuckled. "I'm fairly certain you're not insane, by any reasonable definition. But I'm happy to delve a bit deeper on your behalf."

"Thank you, Father."

"All part of the job," he assured her. "And when do I get to formally meet your daughter?"

Liz thought for a moment. "If you're not above making a house call, come have dinner with us tomorrow evening?"

Felix smiled again. "That sounds lovely. I'll drop by at six, and maybe have some more information for you, depending on what I can dig up." He handed her a business card. "Here's my card. My cell is on there, just in case."

Liz giggled at the mental image of a brown-robed monk with the ecumenical bald head, holding an '80s-era brick phone to his ear. "Wow. Priests are a lot more tech-friendly than when I was little."

Felix reached into his top desk drawer and produced a decade-old flip phone, laughing. "We're getting there." Putting down the old device, he leaned forward in a conspiratorial whisper. "You know, we even use the internet from time to time."

Liz dropped the card into her purse and smiled. "Okay. Tomorrow at six. Thank you, Father."

Liz exited, shutting the door behind her.

Felix took a moment, glancing at his Army photo and remembering. Then he turned to a file cabinet behind his desk and opened one of

the drawers. Peering over his glasses, he began thumbing through the folders inside.

"Who are you, Sister?"

CHAPTER 11

Liz entered her bathroom in a sage green terrycloth robe as the late afternoon sun poured through the gauzy curtains in canted beams. Turning the shower handle, she shed the bathrobe, and stepped into the tile enclosure, quietly shutting the glass door behind her.

Leaning forward with her head under the spout, she began to move the warm water around on her body in slow caresses. She hugged slender arms around a frame which had been curvier in years past, now beginning to feel the effects of gravity.

Jase had loved that body, at every stage, in every condition. He could never keep his hands off Liz, even throughout her pregnancy with Audrey. He was always grabbing her ass, or coming up behind her to cup her breasts, or softly bite the crook of her neck.

And she loved it.

Especially the neck thing. It was like the fast track to Quickie Town.

She loved how physical he was, how he demonstrated his love and desire for her every day they were together.

God, she missed that, missed his touch.

Missed any touch.

Liz had heard the term "skin hunger" in the first and only bereavement group meeting she'd attended back at Pendleton. At the time, she didn't know how apt the name was for the condition she was now feeling so acutely.

Human beings were social animals. Physical touch triggered the release of various mood stabilizing endorphins, while reducing stress hormones. Humans literally needed physical touch to be healthy. She hadn't really been paying attention at the time, her brain still in that state of shock and fog. The time in the early stages of grief, when you're not supposed to make any Big Life Decisions...like moving across the country.

Skin hunger. She was feeling it now.

Hugging her daughter was all well and good, but it was no replacement for the embrace of her mate.

As the shower filled with steam and mist from the hot water, Liz let her hands begin to explore her own body for the first time in months. Letting the water cascade down over her shoulders and the gentle curves of her breasts and stomach, she closed her eyes and took a deep, calming breath. Each hand found the protrusion of her hip bones and followed the indent downward in that familiar V shape.

As the fingers of her right hand pushed through the patch of thick hair on her pubic mound, spreading the delicate flesh, a third hand reached out from the mist. It was powdery white, delicate, and feminine. It rose slowly upward from her belly, pale fingers touching between her breasts, to her throat. Liz shuddered as the hand caressed and played over her neck and jaw, touching that place in the crook of her shoulder where Jason could get her going with a single kiss or a subtle bite.

The hand suddenly clamped down over her nose and mouth, aging and withering at the same time. The hand and arm instantly erupted in wounds—words haphazardly cut into the skin. Blood seeped and oozed from the ghastly carvings, running down Liz's belly to her legs and down the drain. Her eyes blinked open and grew wide in terror as her own hands raced to grasp the third hand clamped over her mouth.

She couldn't breathe.

Struggling with the ghostly hand, screaming in muffled cries, Liz thrashed within the shower stall, toppling plastic shampoo bottles from corner shelves. The hand gripped her jaw, whipping her around by her head, and out of the shower spray.

To the shoulder of Sister Beatrice.

The woman was carved in bleeding words across every inch of her body. The hand over Liz's nose and mouth relaxed, and Liz smelled carrion. Fresh earth. Death. She leaned in close to Liz's ear, whispering, *"Shhhhhh..."*

Liz tried to look backward and scream in fear, but couldn't produce more than a stifled murmur. She flung her body to the side with every ounce of strength she could muster, shattering the glass shower door in a million tiny shards.

She erupted from her sleep, clawing her way to a sitting position as if fighting the hand pulling her backward from her dream.

The bedside clock read 3:17 a.m. The prescription bottle sat open on the nightstand.

A distant *thump* echoed from downstairs, and Liz was suddenly alert.

She glanced quickly at the clock, then turned her attention toward the open bedroom door. As she listened, another *thump* hit her ears, as if someone were going through the kitchen cupboards.

Liz sat upright in her boy shorts and USMC t-shirt, swung her legs over the edge of the bed, and peered out through the door into the hall.

A man in Marine desert fatigues passed by the gap in the doorway, heading downstairs.

"Hello?" Her eyes blinked wide and she scampered out of bed after the mystery person. She got halfway down the stairs and stopped, listening for more noises. "Hello!"

Another *thump* set her feet moving again.

She hit the bottom landing and crossed through the living room to the kitchen, where a gasp escaped her throat and she froze in place.

Standing across the center island in his clean desert camo fatigues was Lt. Jason Charles.

Her hand went to cover her mouth, and she smelled herself. "Oh my God."

Jason looked up and smiled at her. "Hi, Baby."

Liz teared up instantly—she could hardly croak the words—"Jase? How...?"

"Do I get a hug or what?" The handsome Marine went to the front of the island and opened his arms. Liz ran to him, wrapping her husband in a tight embrace. They kissed passionately.

"Oh God, I missed you," Liz whispered through a veil of tears.

"I miss you too."

As they kissed, Liz closed her eyes, lost in a deluge of heartache and saline.

Not noticing the sudden change—

—into the burned, bloody, wounded Captain in shredded fatigues.

She opened her eyes and jumped back, startled in terror.

Jase fell back against the lower cabinets, as if propped on the pile of bricks and car debris in Kandahar. Bloody smears and handprints covered the counters and surfaces of the kitchen. Entrails and viscera were strewn across the floor. The body of Caleb Douglas, clad in his dirty school uniform, lay dead and limp in the crook of his elbow.

Jason's hemorrhaged eyes implored Liz and he tried to raise his single blackened, burned arm, smoldering with missing fingers. "You have to be strong."

Liz slid to her knees on the kitchen floor, weeping, lost in emotional torment. "Jase... no...baby..."

"Help them."

The hiss of the imperative echoed in her mind.

Help them.

Liz thrashed awake, drenched in sweat and sobbing.

The clock read 3:17 a.m.

Liz glanced at the open doorway to see Audrey in an oversize t-shirt, looking concerned. Jase's dog tags hung around her neck.

"Mom? You okay?"

Liz tried to calm down, with marginal success. "Come on in, honey."

Audrey entered, climbing into Liz's bed.

"Just had a nightmare. That's all."

"About dad?"

"Yeah."

Audrey sighed. "Me too."

"Really?"

Audrey snuggled in at her mother's side. "Sometimes I dream about him being hurt."

Liz frowned. "You do?"

"Yeah. But it's only a bad dream, right? You said he's in heaven now."

Liz crushed Audrey to her in a side embrace. "Oh, sweetie, I believe that with all my heart."

"He's still watching over us. I can feel it."

Liz cuddled close to her daughter as they both settled down to sleep. "So can I."

Blinking back tears, she held onto Audrey with everything she had.

CHAPTER 12

Friday.

Day 5.

Liz, in jeans, a worn military fatigue shirt and her hair in a ponytail, wandered among the well-ordered and empty desks of Howard Stonewall's classroom. The painted master-pieces of Audrey and her fellow tweens were pinned up around the room, or hung drying on clotheslines made of craft yarn.

The bespectacled and bookishly-attractive young teacher leaned a hip on his desk, flipping through a file folder. His light green sweater and tan bow tie complimented a pair of khaki Dockers and autumn-themed argyle socks.

Meandering to a window that looked over the empty play area, Liz peered out to where Audrey sat in the middle of three swings, reading a comic book, drifting lazily in the black rubber seat.

Finally, Mr. Stonewall put the folder down on his desk with a slap that jarred Liz out of her fog.

"She's an extremely bright and precocious young lady, Mrs. Charles."

Liz managed a thin smile, and Howard continued.

"In fact, her vocab test this first week had the highest score in the class. All correct plus the extra credit."

"That's good to know," Liz replied blankly.

The teacher shifted uncomfortably, unsure how to raise the topic.

"But...you see...she's not very sociable with the other children. And while I admit it's great that she doesn't disrupt class with a lot of talking, it's...well it's just a red flag for me as a teacher."

Liz scuffed the toe of her Reebok trainers on the linoleum floor, tapping at a splatter of paint that had dried years ago. "She's always been an introvert, Mr. Stonewall."

Howard tried to frame his reaction without confrontation. "And that's absolutely fine, Mrs. Charles. I get it. Being twelve, being a military kid, and going through the loss your family has gone through...I just hope we can facilitate some help for her fragile emotional state..."

He droned on, his voice fading into the background.

Liz glanced wistfully out the window at Audrey, who has been joined by Caleb on the swing to her right.

The young girl still wore her school uniform from the day, and had her father's dog tags around her neck.

Caleb, in his vintage shorts-and-blazer combo, sat forward as Audrey read her copy of *Torchlight Lullaby*. "Your mom lets you read comic books?"

Audrey kept her eyes on the page. "Sure. Why?"

"I have to sneak 'em," Caleb said softly.

Audrey regarded the boy for a moment. "That's too bad."

"Which is your favorite?"

Although she could have held a TED Tak on the subject, Audrey decided to keep the answer brief, for Caleb's sake. "I like a lot of alternative stuff and manga, mostly. *Torchlight Lullaby, Sprecken, Glass Wings, Bleach...*"

Caleb glazed over and looked away. "I don't know those. Mine's *Batman*."

Audrey closed her graphic novel and offered it over to her friend. "Well it's not *Batman*, but you can read mine if you want."

Suddenly Caleb glanced at the boiler room door, apprehensive. Standing at the top of the outside stairwell, the black and white habited form of Sister Beatrice glared at them.

"N-no, that's okay..." Caleb stammered. "The Sister doesn't like them. I'll get punished."

Audrey looked up to see the nun watching them across the empty playground. "She can't punish you—it's after school. And reading comics isn't sinful..."

"She's gonna punish me." The young boy became agitated and a single tear streaked his left cheek.

Audrey frowned. "Don't be scared, Caleb."

Caleb looked at her, a tragic look of primal fear on his pale face. "Help me."

Liz turned away from the classroom window, interjecting now that Howard had finally trailed off. "I won't pretend that we haven't been through a kind of personal hell, Mr.

Stonewall. Losing a spouse is..." She trailed off, then shifted gears. "But the move has been rough on top of everything else, and it may take Audrey more than a week to get settled in here."

Howard nodded agreement. "For sure. I hope the drawing therapy helps with her processing."

Liz folded her arms across her chest, laughing sarcastically. "Oh yeah, those drawings are a real dinnertime conversation starter, let me tell you." She gestured a thumb out the window to the playground. "But it's not like she hasn't made *any* friends. She's gotten pretty close to that boy Caleb."

Howard paused, squinting at her. "I'm not familiar with a Caleb."

Liz grunted, fed up. "Gaah! Enough with that. Mrs. Phillips already said you didn't have a Caleb Douglas here, but she's talking to him on the swings right now."

Howard strode to the window to look out onto the playground.

Audrey sat alone on the swings. The one to her right twisted gently on its chains in the wind.

"I'm sorry, there doesn't seem to be anyone with her."

Liz turned to the window to see for herself —Caleb was gone.

Audrey glanced up to see her mom in the classroom. She waved. Liz returned the gesture.

"He probably just left," she presumed. "And on that note..."

Howard Stonewall passed her a file folder with a few scored tests and some graded homework inside. "Do keep in touch, Mrs. Charles. If there's anything I can do, or if you want to talk over coffee sometime..."

"Thank you, Mr. Stonewall, but my dance card is full." Liz took the folder, collecting her things by the classroom door.

Howard was immediately uncomfortable. "I wasn't...I didn't mean..."

"We have to go. Dinner's not gonna cook itself."

Then Liz was gone, disappearing into the main hallway toward the exit, and a dinner date with a priest.

CR

Early evening sunlight bathed the Charles home in hues of orange and gold. The air hung in misty banks that smelled of wood smoke and cedar. Pumpkin spice was everywhere and in everything. Autumn was officially in full swing. Before long, snow would be on the ground, and then people would be Christmas shopping and playing Whamageddon.

The first Christmas without Jase would be hard. The first *anything* without Jase would be hard. Hell, just living every new day without him felt like a Herculean task.

A long shadow fell across the front walkway, and the rhythmic sound of footsteps on concrete approached from its place of origin. A lanky man in black slacks and a matching wool overcoat approached, stepping up to the front door and knocking a strong rhythm.

The door opened from within, revealing Liz in a well-used cooking apron.

She smiled, wiping her hands on the apron and shaking his hand. "Father! You made it! Come on in!"

Liz beckoned Felix into the house, accepting the bottle of wine he offered and reading the illustrated label. Houdini's Mysterious Disappearing Wine, a Napa Valley Cabernet Sauvignon of 2014 vintage. This priest didn't mess around.

It also happened to be Jase's favorite.

"Looks like you're getting settled in," said Father Felix, glancing around the humble but well-designed interior.

"Slowly but surely."

Felix followed Liz into the kitchen and dining area to discover Audrey drawing at the table, still in her uniform and her dad's dog tags.

"Aha. This must be Audrey…"

The young girl looked up at the priest with a neutral expression. "Hi."

"Audrey, honey," Liz called from the kitchen, "I need you to gather up your art stuff and move it to the other room. We'll be eating in just a few minutes."

The priest leaned over the table and gave the girl a snaggle-toothed smile. "I'm Father Felix. Nice to meet you."

Audrey began to stack her pencils and markers for storage. "Are you here to tell them to go away?"

"Them?" Felix looked confused.

"The angry ones."

Felix was unsure what to say. He glanced at Liz in the kitchen as she readied the meal, then back at Audrey, somewhat shaken by what she'd been drawing: A girl and boy—

clearly Audrey and a friend—threatened by a large, black cloud monster with glowing red eyes, and a scary-looking nun. He knew he would address the nun's identity with Liz later in the evening. The amorphous black form, however, had triggered something deep in his gut. A fear he hadn't felt in a long time.

"Are those the angry ones?"

Audrey gave a simple nod. "They don't want us here."

Felix smirked. "Well, we'll just have to see about that, won't we?" He gave Audrey a sly wink, then turned toward the kitchen to join Liz. "Here, I'll open the wine."

CHAPTER 13

Hours passed. The night lay cool and dark like a threadbare shawl around the quiet Tudor house at the end of the country lane.

Father Felix sat alone at the dining table, perusing several of Audrey's more disturbing drawings while Liz went through the bedtime routine with her daughter. He noticed the recurring motif of the giant black monster and ghostly nun, along with the heartbreaking depictions of her father's death.

War truly is hell.

Or rather, he thought, quoting Hawkeye Pierce from the old *M*A*S*H* television series, *"War isn't Hell. War is war, and Hell is Hell. And of the two, war is a lot worse."* As a man who had firsthand knowledge of both, Felix was inclined to agree. *"There are no innocent bystanders in Hell, but war is chock full of them."*

Amen, Hawkeye. Amen.

He grabbed his wine glass, noticed it was empty, then reached for one of two open bottles on the table, revealing it to be likewise empty when he tried to pour.

Liz entered from the living room, automatically ducking into the kitchen to grab a third bottle from the counter. She took a seat at the table, using the bottle opener like a pro. "So, tanker, huh? What was that like? Unless you'd rather not talk about it..."

Father Felix offered a wistful smile, leaning back in his chair. "No, it's fine. I don't regret the experience, mostly because of the path it set me on."

"What do you mean?" Liz asked, popping the cork and dispensing a generous pour in each glass.

Felix closed his eyes, reliving the sensations of having experienced hell more closely than most living people. "I was in Bravo Company, First Tiger Brigade. Our tank was called 'Blasty Boys'." He cracked a slight smile. "Know what the motto for the Second Armored Division is? 'Hell on Wheels'. Might be the most ironic slogan in the military." The smile faded as he drifted back in time. "When we rolled into Iraq, we were an endless line of armor as far as the eye could see, like medieval knights on horseback. The well fires made the sky dark as night, and exploding vehicles lit up that black sky like cheap fireworks."

He opened his eyes to fix on a point in space a mile away. "We were less than a week in-country, when something came out of the desert and started stalking us at night. It would pace back and forth in front of the sentries like some kind of beast. Night vision... IR...nothing picked it up. But we could *feel* it. It left no tracks, just sort of moved in the shadows—making a noise like garbled voices on the radio."

"My God," Liz gasped, almost a whisper.

"I don't think so," he replied. "Not any god I recognize, anyway. We set up extra night watches to try to bag it. This fella, 'Brushfire' we called him...full-blooded Lakota Sioux... stereotype aside, he was our best tracker. Rarely slept. *He* couldn't even find the thing. Every time we thought we'd cornered it, it always showed up behind us. Followed us for a month or more, keeping just beyond the reach of the sentries, and playing cat-and-mouse with our crew..."

Liz took a deep breath, wide-eyed, as Felix went on.

"Then early one morning, 'Squibbs', our gunner, was out taking a leak in a bomb crater near some burned-out vehicles—a sedan and a couple of light pickups. He started to hear the sound...the garbled radio voices. He turned around and saw...whatever it was, kind of a dark cloud gathering inside the cab of one of the trucks. We were moving out and I was ordered to bring him back to the tank. I watched him take out his sidearm and approach the open passenger window. The dark cloud in the cab was opaque—not quite *solid*, but it blacked out everything behind it. Squibbs put his pistol through the window opening and fired until his clip was empty. Then he screamed."

Liz listened in rapt attention, interjecting softly, "What happened?"

"I ran down the embankment and got there in time to see that his right arm had gone limp, cold to the touch, and his pistol was lying on the ground, slide open. He said his arm had suddenly frozen—gone completely numb, and he couldn't feel or move anything below the shoulder. I picked up his sidearm and helped him back to the tank, but whatever it was didn't like that I'd come to the rescue. I looked back one last time and could have sworn I saw a pair of red eyes like burning coals glaring back at me. Squibbs didn't regain feeling in his right arm for another forty-eight hours."

Liz took a deep breath. "What was it, do you think?"

Felix shrugged, still staring through his wine glass, squinting into the past. "I didn't know what it was at the time. It wasn't us. It wasn't them. It wasn't...human. It was as close to pure evil as I've ever come." He finally looked at her, adding, "And it followed me home."

A shiver shot down Liz's spine at the revelation, and Felix tried to wrap up his tale without delving too much farther down the rabbit hole.

"But after some time, I discovered its name: *Eligos*. One of the so-called great dukes of Hell. In some of the apocrypha, he appears as a dark shadow, or an armored knight on horseback—and you remember how this story started. He's known for discovering hidden things, knows how any war will play out, and how to set soldiers against one another."

Liz clutched her wine glass to her chest, absolutely riveted to the priest's tale. "So this...Eligos...was just camped out in the desert, waiting for someone to latch onto?"

"What better place to find a warrior to feed on than in the land of the Crusades? Where wars have been fought for centuries over material greed, land, oil, or what name to call God?" Felix's tone was laden with sadness and futility as he caressed the inside of his left wrist.

Liz noticed, realizing that every time she'd seen Father Felix, he'd been in long sleeves. She found herself wondering what was hidden beneath the cuff of that black shirt.

"Anyway," he continued, "I learned how to defend myself, and how to...dispel the darkness. At least, to keep it away from the doorstep." He winked at Liz. "So far, so good."

"Holy shit." Too late, Liz realized her slip of the tongue, and put a hand over her mouth in embarrassment.

Father Felix chuckled under his breath. It was time. "Speaking of which, you're gonna need that wine..."

Liz plucked the glass by the stem and put it to her lips, taking a sip. "What did you find out?"

"There was in fact a Sister Beatrice employed at St. Francis school from 1945 to 1958."

Liz frowned. "So what's she still doing hanging around the school?"

"Looking for a cemetery, maybe. She died in 1963."

"I'm sorry...died?"

"At a psychiatric hospital in Manhattan."

"But how is that possible?"

Felix pointed at one of Audrey's pictures. "If this is who you saw, then I suspect you're picking up on some very old baggage."

Liz stared at Felix incredulously, but the priest forged ahead.

"Two young boys, students, went missing in 1958 near the school. The janitor was implicated in the disappearances. The school was closed for two years and Sister Beatrice was transferred to a diocese clear across-country. No bodies were ever found."

Liz shuddered again. "Was...um, was the janitor a big guy?"

Felix opened a file folder on the table and handed a photocopy of a newspaper article to Liz. Featured was a photo of the man she encountered in the school basement.

"That's one word for it," Felix said. "Andrew Hurst. Close to seven foot and three-hundred-fifty pounds. Had some sort of unspecified behavior disorder, but of course I can't find any of his medical records to see what."

Liz perused the newspaper article, sighing as her stomach sank and flipped over on itself. "Oh... oh no... That's the man I saw in the basement."

"Are you sure?"

"There's no mistaking that face..."

Felix nodded. "No charges were ever brought, but Hurst was committed to Agnews Developmental Center in Santa Clara, California, where he died in 1970."

Liz took a serious gulp of wine, as Felix thumbed through the folder for another photo. Producing an old black and white portrait, he passed it to Liz. "This is the nun?"

Liz looked down at the photo of Sister Beatrice and shivered again. "Yes." Though the picture had clearly been taken early in her career as a nun, and the woman she'd seen more recently was considerably less beatific, there was no mistaking it as Sister Beatrice.

Felix flipped through his folder, passing a third photo across the table. "And is this your daughter's playmate?"

As Liz peered at the vintage school portrait of Audrey's friend, her hand flew to cover her mouth, gasping when she saw. "Caleb Douglas!"

Felix slid an almost identical photo to her. "Caleb Edgerton, Douglas Edgerton." One photo showed a happy smile with wary eyes looking from beneath parted hair, while the other captured a more subdued look, and hair parted the opposite direction.

Felix continued. "Twin brothers, age twelve. These were taken in 1957, the year before they disappeared." He leaned back, allowing himself a big sip from his wine glass. "Congratulations, Liz. Within 48 hours of moving to a new town, you've managed to dredge up a scandal this community has tried to forget for sixty years."

Liz chuckled in disbelief. "How does one gal get so lucky?"

Felix regarded her thoughtfully for a moment. She earnestly wanted his advice, and the wine had loosened him up enough to let her in on some of the stagecraft not available to laypersons. "Well," he began, "according to Rome, God permits the souls of the departed to appear to the living as a means to their salvation."

Liz was dubious. "What do *you* think?"

"I think anyone who thinks they have the rules figured out has limited God in doing so."

Liz nodded, satisfied with the non-committal answer.

The priest continued. "Ultimately, whether it's a demonic presence, or restless souls trying to communicate, you've clearly been singled out for a purpose."

"Great," Liz complained, rolling her eyes.

Felix's voice was soft, his smile genuine. "Don't worry. Whatever it is, you won't face it alone."

"Yeah. I'm BFFs with a spiritual kung fu master."

"I was just gonna say 'God's on our side', but I like the kung fu."

A moment passed between them.

Liz was a bit flushed from the wine and the first male company she'd had since losing her husband.

Felix smiled at her again, rising from the table. "I should go. It's late. I've taken up too much of your evening." Pointing at the open file folder, he added, "You can keep this..."

Liz stood to follow his exit. "It was nice, if not a bit traumatic. What's next?"

"You can poke around online, see if what I gave you leads anywhere. I have some contacts back east digging into the records. We'll see what they come up with."

Liz shadowed Felix to the door, helping him into his jacket. "Are you gonna be okay walking home?"

Felix produced a medium Maglite from his jacket pocket. "Let there be light," he joked. He smiled at the attempt, but returned to a serious note. "Call if you need anything." One last somewhat awkward pause elapsed, then, "Oh, uh, dinner was lovely."

Felix turned to go, and Liz shut the door behind him, turning the deadbolt and heading for the staircase to her bedroom. She gasped as she hit the first riser, taken aback by the sight of Audrey standing at her bedroom door, wearing her father's dog tags and glaring down chillingly at her mother.

"Audrey. What are you—?"

"Dad says they don't like us." The voice was part Audrey, part something else.

Liz gingerly made her way up the stairs to her daughter. "Who doesn't like us, sweetie?"

Audrey was shivering. "Dad says it's too late." That two-part voice again, as if someone was mocking her in their deepest register from another room.

Gathering her daughter to her side and hugging her, Liz ushered Audrey back to her room. "Were you having another dream, honey?"

Audrey pushed away from Liz and gave the same wild-eyed glare. The distant second voice was now a roar. "I'm not kidding, Mom! Dad says Father Felix is poking a hornet's nest! We could have just left, but now we have to finish what we started!" Abruptly, she turned on her heel and stormed off to her room, slamming the door.

Liz could only stare at the closed bedroom door in slack-jawed surprise.

CHAPTER 14

The file folder slapped down on the bed-spread. Liz's laptop screen flipped up and she began to type into the browser search bar. Pixelated results began to fill the screen immediately: articles on the child disappearances of 1958—

"EDGERTON TWINS MISSING"

—references to the school's financial hardships and the transfer of Andrew Hurst to a mental hospital two states away.

Several results simply backed up the information Father Felix had relayed earlier, but she kept coming back to the reports of Hurst's association with the abductions.

"ST. FRANCIS CUSTODIAN SUSPECTED"

A beaded rosary dangled from Liz's left hand as she worked. Her fingers absently caressed the beads as she scanned the screen and file copies through her cheap pharmacy reading glasses.

The photos were spread out on Liz's bed:

Sister Beatrice.

Andrew Hurst.

Caleb Edgerton.

Douglas Edgerton.

Liz typed into the search window: WHY DO GHOSTS APPEAR TO PEOPLE, and the results began to scroll:

"Sensing Ghosts and Presences | Journal of Modern Psychology by Fr. Felix Connelly, PhD"

Scientific articles, news stories and blog posts appeared, and Liz scanned through each one, collecting details and filling in gaps.

"Possible explanations for a sensed presence include...altered sensations and states of consciousness induced by changes in brain chemistry triggered by stress..."

"Seeing ghosts may also be triggered by the 'agency-detection mechanisms'..."

Liz typed FATHER FELIX CONNELLY into the search window, watching the results fill up the screen.

"DESERT STORM VET COUNSELS AFGHAN WAR SOLDIERS WITH PTSD"

"USING FAITH AND SCIENCE, SOLDIER PRIEST HELPS RETURNING VETS"

"Exorcising evil with a cross and a psych degree—Father Connelly is a new kind of crusader..."

"REAL LIFE EXORCIST HELPS LOCAL BOY"

"It's not all spinning heads and spewing pea soup these days. A New Rochelle man, Felix Connelly, a Gulf War veteran with a psych degree who joined the clergy in 1994, has made a name for himself..."

His author photo popped up—a younger man with that same sand-blasted face and those intense eyes. Even in black and white, they stared out of the screen like lasers, following her. Piercing. Probing.

Then the search results for ELIGOS filled the screen, and her mouth fell open.

"Eligos (also Abigor or Eligor)..."

"...also known as the 'Great Duke of Hades'..."

"...a highly respected demon due to his deep knowledge of warfare."

Article after article described the entity as a master strategist, famed for his victories during the First War in Heaven, able to glean enemy tactics even before a battle. Some described the amorphous black shadow Felix had described encountering in the desert. Some as an armored knight—a probable throwback to the Medieval period, when the Crusades were underway.

Then there was his mount, a demonic horse made from skeletal remains, with the feet of a lion, and the tail and wings of a dragon. Apparently a gift from the demon Beelzebub, it was known as the "Steed of Abigor". Astride this hellish beast, the master of warfare led sixty legions of demons in battle.

She'd hit the jackpot, and read until her eyesight went blurry, even behind the cheap glasses. Within twenty minutes, Liz went from hair-standing-on-end to curled in the familiar fetal position, unconscious.

She still clutched the rosary in her left hand. File copies lay spread out on the bed next to her, along with her glasses. The light from her laptop screen saver waved and flickered over her slumbering form until it timed out and, like her, went to sleep.

⌘

Saturday.

Day 6.

The simple lines of the brick Tudor home standing out from the morning mist made the place seem far more isolated than it was. It could just as easily have been the gothic mansion from a Victorian ghost story as a quiet suburban home at the end of a residential street. A deeper chill had set in, one which seeped into the bones and made chins quiver and teeth chatter despite themselves.

Audrey sat on the living room floor by the coffee table, decimating a snack of sliced apple and peanut butter, reading an open comic book next to the plate. A warm fire roared in the hearth, but she couldn't hear the crackle over the angst of My Chemical Romance in her earbuds.

Liz sat on the sofa nearby, warming herself under a blanket while alternating between tapping the laptop keyboard and sipping coffee. She peered through her reading glasses at the screen, still researching. Or, rather, researching *again*.

Audrey removed her earbuds and turned to Liz. "You and Father Felix drank a lot last night," she observed innocuously.

Liz snapped out of her focus on the screen, looking chastened and more than a little hungover. "We had a lot to talk about."

Audrey pondered her mother's non-answer. "About Sister Beatrice?"

"Among other things."

"Like what?"

The sarcastic portion of Liz's brain unleashed a host of possibilities: *Oh, you know. A double homicide from a half-century ago. Ghosts. The Demon of War. The usual stuff.* "It's complicated," she said quietly.

Audrey paused, untangling her earbud wires. "Are we going to service tomorrow?"

"Sure," said Liz, regarding her daughter with a hint of suspicion.

"Cool." Audrey flipped a page in her comic as Liz went back to her computer screen and coffee.

Something moved at the bottom of the stairwell.

Audrey looked up to see Caleb creeping silently up the stairs. She stood, making sure it was a large enough movement to distract her mother. "I'm gonna go draw."

Liz frowned, confused. "You can draw out here if you want."

"Nah," said Audrey, gathering her comic and snack plate. "Just want to be alone for awhile."

"Rinse your plate and leave it in the sink," Liz reminded her. "I don't want to be scrubbing dried-on peanut butter..."

There was the sound of running tap water and a ceramic clank from the kitchen, and Audrey leaned over the back of the sofa to kiss her mother as she crossed back through the living room to the staircase.

Pausing briefly at the top landing, Caleb ducked into the spare third bedroom, which Audrey had claimed as an art studio on account of its south-facing window.

Climbing the stairs quickly, Audrey entered the spare room after Caleb, glancing around for any sign of him. But the boy was gone.

She pulled open the closet door to find nothing but hanging clothes.

Going to the light of the window, Audrey pulled an old chair up to her father's old drafting table. Jason had been a budding cartoonist in his youth, obsessed with comic books. He'd shared that passion with Audrey. She grabbed one of the drawing pads from the stack next to the table, picking up a pencil and closing her eyes.

Caleb approached silently behind her, putting a hand on Audrey's shoulder. She seemed not to notice, but opened her eyes and started to draw in earnest.

Time seemed to skew as forms began to take shape on the paper: the giant black presence and the nun, the hulking janitor, and the young boy—followed by another identical boy. Her tiny hand flew across the surface, filling in the details. She found a red pencil and began to saturate the mouths of the two boys in the picture. Words began to appear.

The spare room's door creaked open. Sister Beatrice loomed in the corner by the open doorway.

The frightening images continued to take shape on the page.

Suddenly the nun swooped in behind the girl, as if on an under-cranked movie camera. She leaned in close, a pale hand reaching up toward the severe line of a mouth.

"Shhhhhh."

Audrey startled, turning around to check behind herself. Sister Beatrice was gone and the bedroom door was closed. Audrey turned back around to look at the drawing and startled again at what she'd drawn. She swallowed hard and tore the sheet out of the pad, folding it in quarters and stuffing it into her backpack.

CHAPTER 15

Liz stood in the corner of the kitchen, drying plates and putting them away in cabinets as fast as Audrey washed and stacked them in the wire rack.

Audrey appeared lost in thought, leaning over the basin of warm water from her vantage atop a folding step stool.

"You okay?" Liz asked, wiping water from a fork and sliding it into the silverware drawer.

Audrey shrugged in her preteen way, suds up to her elbows. "Just thinking."

"About what?"

"I like Father Felix."

"Yeah?"

"He's nice," Audrey smiled, rinsing a table knife and sticking it edge-down in the flatware pocket of the dish drainer.

Liz smiled wistfully, allowing Audrey to build up some backlog in the drainer before grabbing the stragglers to dry. "Yeah."

Audrey shook the suds from her hands, having scoured the last of the eating utensils. "He reminds me of Grandpa."

"He's a bit younger than Grandpa," Liz observed.

Audrey pulled the stopper from the drain and stepped down from the stool, wiping her hands on a clean towel. "I miss Grandma and Grandpa."

"So do I, sweetie," Liz frowned.

Audrey turned, looking Liz in the eye. "I miss Dad."

Liz caught a sob in her throat, tears immediately forming. "Oh, Audrey honey, so do I."

Suddenly distraught, Audrey clamped her eyes shut. Something was here. Something was compelling her sadness and grief. Compelling her to lash out. "I want to move back home."

Liz found her strength momentarily. "Audrey, stop it. This *is* your home."

The look Audrey gave her in response was half her little girl, half something of pure, seething hate. "No it's *not!* But dad says we can't go until we finish!"

"What do you mean?" Liz demanded, unsettled by Audrey's demeanor. "Finish what?"

Audrey looked down and noticed she'd knotted the dish towel into a solid ball. The anger was taking over. "I don't know, but I wanna go home! I hate it here, *I hate it!*"

There it was again—the look, and that tone that wasn't just her own daughter's voice. Liz had reached her limit. "That is *enough*, young lady!"

The girl kicked the step tool aside and let the full fury of her anger fly.

"I hate this house! I wanna go home!"

She stormed out of the kitchen and through dining room, leaving a shocked and bewildered Liz alone in the kitchen, eyes welling with tears.

Liz dabbed her eyes with the used towel, suddenly overwhelmed with a realization. Her daughter wasn't wrong. In fact, she'd been right all the time. In Liz's desire to remove them from the triggers of their grief, she'd separated them from their friends and family, from their support network. From the people who knew them best, and wanted the best for them.

She should have known better.

Everyone knew a cross-country move wasn't something to be undertaken while in the throes of grief.

Everyone but Liz, apparently.

Strong, stoic, thick-headed Liz. Faithful Catholic. Marine Corps wife.

Oorah.

☙

Father Felix sat at his desk, reclining with his gray-socked feet propped to one side of his computer screen. His glasses rested on his forehead, fingers rubbing weary eyes and temples. It had been a long day, and much of it non-productive.

Bishop Michael O'Rourke, his former Army chaplain and contact at the Archdiocese of New York, was probably not in his office on Saturday, thus there would likely be no response to his email before Monday.

He sat up and stretched, cracking his neck and preparing to leave to go home.

From within the sanctuary, there was a soft rasping sound, and a faint whiff of sulfur. Felix peered out the open office door into the church, gauging the darkness. Somewhere within the flickering candlelight of the sanctuary, a shadow moved.

Suddenly an email notification pinged from the computer, drawing his attention back to the screen. He peered through his glasses at a display full of photo attachments and information. Snippets of words flashed across their reflective surface.

SUBJECT: RECORD SEARCH - SISTER BEATRICE - ANDREW HURST

Felix,

I happened to duck into the office today to clear some work off my plate before the retreat next weekend, and saw your email. What have you gotten yourself into, my son?

As you gathered from the available news records online, two students at your St. Francis school went missing in 1958, and the janitor, Andrew Hurst, was charged with their murders. Hurst was found non compos mentis by the court, and sentenced to be committed at Western State Hospital near Seattle in 1959. He was transferred to Agnews Develop-

mental Center in 1964, and committed suicide in his cell in 1970—slashed his wrists with a stolen box cutter.

As for your Sister Beatrice, brace yourself. Proceed with caution, and be advised the attached photos and video are disturbing. There is a case history that may shed some light on the origins of her particular mental condition. I don't know what afflicted these poor, disturbed souls, whether natural or supernatural in origin, and I don't know what you're digging up out there. Only be careful—if you're going to war again, do not forget to take the Ephesians with you.

Be safe. Go with God.

Your friend,

Mick

Father Felix scanned the text of the email and clicked to open a photo file. His eyes widened in shock, and he was forced to sit back in his chair.

"My God."

☙

The Charles house sat quiet and serene, il-luminated by moonlight and the occasional exterior fixture. One light showed through an upstairs bedroom window, another through the dining room downstairs. The silhouette of Liz moved across the window, exiting the room to ascend the staircase. As she did so, the din-ing room light flickered briefly.

A second silhouette—a woman in flowing robes—suddenly appeared and followed Liz from the room.

Liz climbed the stairs to the second floor, unaware of the second shadow falling on the steps behind her.

Audrey lay in bed, hugging a pillow to her chest, her back to the room.

Liz entered, gently approaching and sitting on the edge of the comforter. "I'm sorry, Au-drey," she said, gingerly laying a hand on Au-drey's shoulder. "You're right. It wasn't fair of me to drag you up here."

Audrey slowly turned over to look at her mother. "Do we have to stay?"

Liz stroked Audrey's cheek. "No, honey. No, we can go home. I'll call Sandra to start the process on Monday. Might take a couple weeks to figure out, and you'll stay in school until we go. Understood?"

Audrey seized Liz around the waist in a tight hug. "I love you, Mom."

"I love you too, sweetie."

CHAPTER 16

The world lay cloaked in a thick autumn mist that crept along the ground like a blanket of vermin. The lone streetlamp outside the old brick Tudor was a diffuse orb, shimmering in a cloud of moths. As Audrey slept peacefully, her father's dog tags rising and falling with each breath, the background whisper of eerie conversation began to emanate from around her. Dialog between souls long departed from the mortal plane, exchanged in hushed, over-lapping snippets of indistinct origin.

The atmosphere became stale, almost oppressive. And one word began to drown out the rest of the whispers.

"Audrey..." began to form in the girl's ear—a young boy's soft voice. "Audrey...come on."

Waking with a start, still clutching her father's dog tags, Audrey raised herself onto her elbows to see Caleb staring at her from the foot of her bed. He wore the same ragged school uniform from the 1950s, dried blood caked around his mouth.

"Audrey...come on," he beckoned without actually speaking, then suddenly bolted from her bedroom.

She slid out of bed and went to the bedroom door. The whispers followed, and so did the earnest address from Caleb.

"Audrey..."

Following the murmured call, Audrey exited her room and padded quietly down the stairs to the front door. She could now see the twins, Caleb and Douglas, standing by the front entry, sporting their identical school uniforms and wearing the same caked blood on their faces. The only visible difference seemed to be that Douglas parted his hair to the right, whereas Caleb let his matted bowl cut cling to his forehead.

The front door was wide open.

Douglas beckoned. "Quickly! Before the Sister comes." Then the boys ducked out the door.

"Audrey..."

Audrey quietly went to the door and followed the two boys outside. She shut the door behind her.

ᚙ

Liz, in pajama bottoms and her trusty USMC night shirt, woke with a start and fumbled through her nightstand drawer but could not find the pills she'd been relying upon to keep her unconscious.

She slid off the edge of the bed, leaving the disorderly pile of file folder, photocopies and actual photos. The small laptop winked on in response to her movement on the mattress, casting a wan light across the rumpled bedspread.

The whispers returned.

Entering the master bathroom, she went to the sink and started the tap. She splashed a couple handfuls of water on her face and dipped her head down to rinse in the water, her hand feeling for the towel on the vanity. She rose back up, drying her face with the towel—

—and when she lowered it from her eyes, she saw her beautiful, perfect husband standing behind her in the mirror's reflection, in desert camo.

"Damnit, Jason," she spat.

The image in the mirror looked hurt. "I'm here, love."

"No you're not," Liz cried, bursting into tears. "Not really."

The apparition moved forward, coming closer to the mirror. Jason's chestnut eyes glimmered under the brim of his field cap. "I'm with you, but you've got to be strong for me."

"I can't!" Liz whined, hiding her face back in the hand towel.

"You can," she heard him say, feeling his hands on her shoulders. "You must."

Again she lowered the towel from her eyes, and now the reflection was that of Jason after the second blast, his face like raw meat, rivulets of blood from head to toe. His fatigues were black and charred. "HELP THEM!"

Liz gasped in terror, whirling around to face him, but he was gone.

"Jase!"

The scuffling of claws on ceramic drew her eye to the corner of the bathroom, to the base of the old steam radiator. A single band of moonlight illuminated a large crow, which pecked and scratched at a seam between the tiles. It hopped from side to side, glancing up at Liz, then pecking intently at the seam. The bird's croaks merged with the whispers.

The whispers became shrieks, then silence.

Liz awoke a second time to see the robed form and malevolent face of Sister Beatrice at the foot of her bed, glowering down over her. In the back of the room stood an imposing figure clad in black armor, two points of fire ember light staring out from a helmed head.

She tried to move, but suddenly felt paralyzed, heavy, as if she weighed several tons.

Or were being held down by an unseen force.

She could scarcely breathe, let alone cry out, but she tried anyway, wheezing a pitiful gasp of alarm. Panic sprouted in her chest and spread through her entire body, flooding her senses with fear and her muscles with useless adrenaline.

The Sister leaned over, her moon face looming out of the dark. One slender talon finger rose to her pursed lips.

"Shhhhhh."

And then the horrible face was gone, the armored figure in the corner was gone, and suddenly Liz could move, the feeling and control returning to her limbs. Thrashing and punching at the air like a fighting dog released from its chain, she scrambled for the bedside light and when she turned it on, no one was there.

The room was empty, except for her.

Her clock read 3:17 a.m.

She picked up the phone and flipped through the file folder to locate Father Felix's card, but then calmed herself and put the phone down.

A knock at the front door jarred her back into a state of panic.

CR

Now clad in Jase's favorite flannel shirt over her night clothes, Liz sprinted downstairs to the entry and peered through the door light with the broken spindle. Surprised, she opened the door to find Father Felix, carrying a tablet computer and uncharacteristically nervous.

"Father? Come in." Liz opened the door to welcome him inside, her own nerves thrumming with excitement and fear. She angled her head toward the kitchen. "I'll make us some tea."

Felix, clearly antagonized, followed her, beginning to pace as he entered the kitchen. "I'm so sorry to intrude at this hour...but I felt it couldn't wait."

Liz nodded, intent on being heard. Her words tumbled out haphazardly. "I was just about to call you. She was here. Sister Beatrice. In the house. She...held me down. I couldn't move or scream. And there was someone...something else, standing behind her. Like an armored knight. And I saw my...husband. I keep seeing Jason."

Felix met her gaze with his own blue-eyed intensity. "I know. I believe you."

"You're kind of scaring me." Liz swallowed, her fight-or-flight instinct rising in her chest.

"You should be scared, Liz."

Liz gave a look of concern, and Felix set the tablet on the counter, wringing his hands as he relayed the information.

"It seems our good Sister came from a rather pitiful background. This would have been during the Depression, in the '30s. Her family was desperately poor, and her father was implicated in several reports of abuse and... molestation."

Liz forgot all about the tea. She gulped again, swallowing dry air. "Oh no…"

Felix took a deep breath, spelling out the next bit of data in plain terms. "Before joining the service of Our Lord, Sister Beatrice was known as Sarah Hurst. Andrew Hurst appears in the records to be the…illegitimate offspring of Sarah—"

He stumbled to finish the sentence, but Liz heard it in her head before he spoke.

And her own father!

"—and her own father." Felix sighed, unwilling to let those words be the end of the story. "Which could explain Andrew's mental condition. After the Edgerton twins disappeared, Beatrice…Sarah…was outspoken in defense of Andrew, which makes sense if he was her son. And also because Andrew was mute." He paused, letting every word sink in. "His tongue had been removed. Cut out."

"Ugh…Oh God." Liz looked suddenly nauseous.

Felix reached for his tablet on the counter and pulled up some files to show her. "I completely understand if you don't want to look."

Liz steadied herself, preparing. He passed her the tablet and she began to page through the photos.

The first few showed a frail and crazed Beatrice relegated to a hospital dressing gown, in various states of dishevelment and conflict with medical staff. The habit usually covered and contained all but a nun's hands and face, but without it she looked like a completely different person. Wiry white hair exploded from a withered scalp, the skin stretched taut over pronounced bones. Lips curled back over craggy teeth.

Liz gasped.

Felix took another deep breath and pushed on. "That's not the half of it. While committed, Sarah stole a utility knife from the hospital janitor and carved a sermon's worth of bible verses into her flesh before attacking an orderly. She died three days later of a systemic infection."

Vivid close-ups of bible verses carved sloppily into human skin suddenly popped up in the photos, and Liz recoiled in horror. One seemed to be repeated over and over:

For God will bring every

deed into judgment, with every

secret thing, whether good or evil.

"Ugh!" Liz shuddered.

Felix sighed. "They're not easy to look at, I know."

Liz re-calibrated her fear and opened the last few files on the tablet.

A black and white photo showed a medical staff member in hospital scrubs splayed on the floor, semi-conscious, bleeding from the mouth. Not just a trace amount, like a lost tooth or split lip—it poured out over swollen lips and a throat gasping for air.

Another showed Sister Beatrice, covered in the medic's blood as well as her own, being wrestled to a bed by two orderlies as they force her to drop the utility knife. An old film movie camera had recorded the same interaction, and Liz played it with the screen maximized.

Beatrice with carved limbs oozing blood, wild hair raging, required two of the largest men Liz had ever seen to restrain her fury. It ended on an image of Sister Beatrice glaring straight into the camera, sinister teeth bared through her newly-tongueless mouth and etched face.

Liz put the tablet down, pushing it back toward Felix. "It's like she's possessed."

The priest looked at her with intent. "Complex PTSD, possible Borderline Personality Disorder, but less than a century ago, the Church would have agreed with you."

Liz shivered. Sarah Hurst had been sexually assaulted...*No, raped—call it what it is.* By her own father. She'd escaped into the haven of the Church, giving her illegitimate and mentally deficient son over into its care, stationed where she could look after him as a benefactor. A protector. But no one could know of their past, know of the sins of Sarah's father. And when the sins of the father were visited upon the son, and Andrew did to the Edgerton twins what Sarah's father had done to her...

Good Lord, Liz thought. *And if she...oh, those poor boys...*

She imagined their panic and tormented cries as Sister Beatrice sawed through their tongues. She heard them screaming and gurgling in agony until Andrew put a sudden and violent end to the horror. Liz had seen Andrew's massive hands in the school basement. It would have been barely an effort to snap their necks.

She wondered which of the brothers Andrew had killed first, thinking that to go last would have had to be unbearable—to be a witness to that brutal assault before it was done to you.

"Here's the other concern," Felix continued, still full of nervous intensity. "Andrew was never baptized, and never had Last Rites when he died. By Church standards, he's a lost soul. And the Edgerton twins. *Probably* murdered, *probably* buried in unhallowed ground."

A chill ran down Liz's spine. "And Sister Beatrice?"

"Maybe she's bound by her father's sin against her, or by her own, in addition to covering up Andrew's crime."

"So are they all...ghosts? If ghosts are real, I mean, can't you banish them to heaven or hell or wherever they're supposed to be?"

Father Felix suddenly became very still, and very serious. His tone softened and he spoke with surgical precision. "Ordinarily, I would say the souls of Sarah, Andrew and the twins were trapped in Limbo, chained to the memory of their former lives, and 'awakened' when you and Audrey arrived in town."

"Ordinarily?" Liz mused. "What's different about this?"

Felix found her eyes, but quickly looked away. "There's a wildcard."

Liz recalled the previous evening of wine and war stories, and the blood drained from her face. "*Eligos,*" she whispered. The armored knight in the corner of her room, standing silently, ominously behind Beatrice as if compelling her to act. The dark form in the background of Audrey's drawings. It all made sense.

Felix nodded. "These are not simple hauntings. Eligos has been inhabiting these lost souls as a way of getting close to you and your daughter."

"But why us?" Liz begged. "Why me?"

"You're a ride-or-die military wife, and you're grieving your husband's death. An awful death. A brutal death. And it's fresh. Your pain and loneliness radiate off you like body heat on a cold day. Audrey too—perhaps even more so. That's an emotional feast for a demon whose whole identity is wrapped up in war and secrets."

Liz rubbed her eyes tiredly. She knew he was right. It occurred to her that Eligos had probably been busy in Afghanistan during the course of America's longest war.

Suddenly she heard a bedroom door open on the second floor. "Hang on a second," she said, heading to the bottom of the stairs. Felix followed as far as the living room.

"Audrey, honey, is everything—"

Her attention was drawn to Audrey's open bedroom door, where Jason stood inside, seemingly in perfect health, peering down at something out of her field of view.

"Jase?"

Liz cleared the stairs three at a time, bursting into Audrey's bedroom, only to find the bed empty and her school binder laying open on the covers. Liz picked up the binder and began to sift through dozens of sheets of paper displaying pencil and marker-scrawled drawings of Sister Beatrice, Andrew, the looming black monster, and bloody death and dismemberment. Punctuating the savage drawings were giant block letters:

HELP THEM. IN THE DARK. IN THE BASEMENT. BE STRONG.

She grabbed Audrey's backpack, pawing through the main pocket, pulling out the folded recent drawing of the monster, the nun and the twin boys, across which was scrawled in red pencil:

WHOSO KEEPETH HIS MOUTH AND HIS TONGUE KEEPETH HIS SOUL FROM TROUBLES

FOR GOD WILL BRING EVERY DEED INTO JUDGMENT, WITH EVERY SECRET THING

Liz clutched it with a handful of the other drawings and ran for the door. She flew down the stairs, frantic as Felix met her.

"She's gone!"

"What?"

"Audrey. She's gone. And her binder was full of these."

Father Felix took the pile of drawings from Liz and sorted through them, frowning. "Does she sleepwalk?"

"No." Liz came to a sudden realization. "Oh shit. When I came to open the door for you, it was unlocked. But I locked it before I went to bed!"

Felix nodded, leading the way out to the car. "She must have left before I arrived. Come on."

CHAPTER 17

Audrey ran in socked feet, the crunch of dry pine needles and maple leaves beneath her. The cold night air was bracing, her breath trailing in a fog as her father's dog tags jangled around her neck.

Up ahead, the Edgerton twins set a quick pace, one occasionally glancing back over his shoulder. They wove through the trees far from the illuminated streets of town. Audrey puffed and sucked in a cool breath, doubling her efforts to keep up.

Time seemed suspended as they cleared the woods and crossed the empty street between the church and the school building, making a bee line toward the concrete stairwell to basement. Audrey could see the door was cracked open, a sliver of eerie orange light creating an upside-down L shape that pierced the dark and the encroaching fog.

She wasn't sure why it was so important to follow the twins. Some kind of conflict had been brewing that required her presence. She knew that playing her part would make it possible to leave this place.

Briefly grasping the dog tags in a freezing hand, she felt her father's presence, and it warmed her a bit.

Then she followed Caleb and Douglas Edgerton down the stairs and into the silently menacing basement.

CR

The black Jeep navigated down the dark neighborhood street, Liz at the wheel while Father Felix dialed 9-1-1 on his mobile phone.

"Yes, this is Father Felix of St. Francis. I'm calling on behalf of one of my parishioners, whose daughter has gone missing."

Liz fought back anguished tears as she kept her eyes on the dark street ahead.

"We don't know exactly," Felix said, answering a question Liz couldn't hear. "Sometime in the last two or three hours. Audrey Charles. Age eleven. Black hair. Brown eyes. About four foot...?" he looked at Liz to fill in the blanks.

"Four foot ten," she muttered, trying valiantly to keep her rising panic under control.

"Four foot ten. Last wearing...?"

"Red pajama pants."

"Red pajama pants. And...?"

"A t-shirt. Some anime design."

"A t-shirt with an anime design on the front..."

Liz suddenly remembered: "Dog tags!"

"What?"

"She's wearing her father's dog tags."

"And she's wearing a set of dog tags. We think she may be heading to St. Francis School. Her mother and I are en route. Yes. Yes, that's right. We can be reached at this number. Alright, thank you."

Father Felix closed his ancient flip-phone, and Liz set her jaw.

"Hang on, sweetie," she muttered under her breath. "Mommy's on her way..."

The Jeep screeched to a stop next to the school playground, and Liz killed the engine.

Glancing toward the ominous brick building, she noticed a lone figure in military fatigues standing vigil at the top of the basement stairs.

Jason.

It made sense. He'd been killed trying to rescue a child from a school bombing. Of course he would journey back from the After-life to help rescue his daughter. Father Felix leaned forward to disengage his seatbelt, and when he leaned back and opened the passenger door, the ghostly soldier was gone.

As Liz and Felix exited the car, a large crow —much like the one Liz had seen in her dream —flapped to a graceful landing atop the metal handrail, peering down the gloomy stairwell for a brief moment before taking flight again, disappearing into the black night sky.

They arrived at the top of the stairs, hearts already pounding. The door at the bottom was open slightly, a strange red-orange glow seeping out from the boiler room beyond. The whispered voices were faint, but could be heard emanating from behind the door.

Liz felt the fear rise in her throat. "Oh God. What do I do?"

Felix pulled his flashlight from his pocket and flicked it on. "Stay close."

Liz followed tentatively as Felix led the way down. Step by cautious step, the two descended into the dank basement, eerie with dim amber light and ethereal whispers. The air was thick and hazy with dust and coal smoke, and the same stench of death and decay permeated every inch of the space.

As they continued, the pitiful sounds of young children crying could be discerned above the whispers. They gradually increased in volume, clawing at every parental fiber of Liz's being. Under the tortured sobbing, another voice could be heard:

"Whoso keepeth his mouth and his tongue keepeth his soul from troubles..."

"Do you hear that?" Liz asked.

Felix paused, cocking his head. "Hear what?"

They stood absolutely still in the dark, the flashlight in the priest's hand their only beacon, until Liz remembered her cell phone. She quickly dug into the chest pocket of the flannel, thumbing the flashlight application on.

As Felix led Liz forward, a scene revealed itself in front of the old boiler, caught in brief flashes of the roaming flashlight beam—

—A pile of bloody clothes crumpled next to the boiler. Wool blazers, long shorts, white underthings, all steeped in blood.

—A stark white sheet as a makeshift shroud, draped across two small bodies leaning slouched against the wall, temple to temple. Blood seeped from locations on the faces, creating the illusion of a pair of mad clown dolls.

—Something moving in the bowels of a passageway.

—Jase's dog tags on the floor.

—Dark spatters of blood everywhere the light fell.

A vision of Sister Beatrice in her black robes, her back to the interlopers, knelt by the boiler in prayer. As Liz's flashlight beam hit her, her head slowly rose and she peered mischievously over her shoulder at Felix.

Liz watched her head move grotesquely in the shadows. "Oh my God, she's here. Sister Beatrice. Do you see her? She's here."

Felix scanned the hazy dark with his own flashlight. "Where?"

"By the boiler."

The priest's flashlight met the one from Liz's phone, combining with it in time to see Sister Beatrice sneering over her shoulder at them. Her eyes were the burning embers Liz had seen within the armored helmet in her bedroom.

"Who's been telling our secrets?"

Liz stared wide-eyed at the scene before her, as Father Felix made the sign of the cross. In doing so, his flashlight roamed to reveal—

—The hulking form of Andrew, standing at the mouth of a low concrete tunnel leading under the school. He was filthy with sweat, soot, and blood. He held Audrey by her head in his massive right arm, his hand clamped around her mouth. His left hand held her left arm behind her back.

Audrey's eyes betrayed mortal fear. Despite her instincts, she'd been lured right to her captors, and now her mom and Father Felix were in terrible danger.

Liz suddenly stepped forward, shrieking: "AUDREY!"

CHAPTER 18

Sister Beatrice's head snapped upright, and Andrew backed away with Audrey into the darkened corridor. The spectral nun turned, her face awash with blood and malice, her eyes wide in frenzy. *"You shouldn't be telling secrets, child. 'For God will bring every deed into judgment, with every secret thing, whether good or evil.'"*

"Eligos." Father Felix stepped forward as he held his own rosary out with the flashlight, reciting from Ephesians: "Be strong in the Lord and in the strength of His might! Put on the full armor of God, so that you will be able to stand firm against the schemes of the devil!"

Distant screams again filled the dark basement.

Sister Beatrice rose creaking to her feet, her head hanging down limply as Father Felix continued his recitation.

"For our struggle is not against flesh and blood, but against the rulers, against the powers, against the world forces of this darkness, against the spiritual forces of wickedness in the heavenly places!"

Her eyes suddenly locked on his, and Sister Beatrice growled like an angry jungle cat, pouncing at Father Felix. In a single action, she batted the flashlight from his hand and flung him across the basement into the wall next to the boiler.

"Hold your tongue, lest the agent of God hold it for you!"

Felix tried to stand, shaken and wheezing for breath, still clasping his rosary.

Liz scrambled toward the dark hallway. Holding her phone in her left hand, she angled the light back toward Father Felix to see Sister Beatrice leap into view in front of her, skeletal finger to her wrinkled lips.

"Shhhhhh!"

A chill of absolute terror shot down her spine, but Liz squinted through her fear. "Where's my daughter?"

The nun's angry grimace became a sinister smile. *"You mean the little one who's been wagging her tongue?"*

"Where's my daughter—give me back my daughter…" Liz turned and fumbled into the dark, away from the apparition. With her phone providing a stark beam of light, she scuffled across the dog tags on the concrete floor and scooped them up, clutching them tightly. "Audrey! I'm coming, honey!"

She turned around in the dark space, unsure of her direction and a little dizzy. Suddenly the nun was back in her beam of light, glaring down at Liz, grinning her sinister grin and producing a tile knife from the folds of her vestments. *"We kept Daddy's secrets…"*

Father Felix stepped between the women, rosary held in front of him. Liz took the opportunity to turn and run.

"Therefore, take up the full armor of God, so that you will be able to resist in the evil day…"

Liz tripped in the dark and fell into a pile of debris, crying out in agony as her left hand and arm were impaled on an assortment of rusty nails and shards of wood. She winced as her right knee took the brunt of the fall, grinding into the concrete. Her phone skittered away into the distance.

Hands shaking, she managed a crouch, though her nerves were on fire. One by one, she extracted the larger pieces from her flesh by feel, every inch a complete torment. Feeling the blood run down her forearm toward her elbow, she slowly gathered her wits and half limped, half crawled toward the glowing phone on the floor in the distance.

"Audrey…" she whimpered quietly, tears of pain clouding her vision in the already hazy basement. Her arm and knee throbbed. She could hear Father Felix continuing his recitation at the other end of the room.

"…and having done everything, to stand firm!"

Sister Beatrice focused her full attention on the priest, plowing past him toward the corridor, knocking him aside for the second time.

Liz plucked her phone from the ground, finding the corner chipped but otherwise undamaged. Despite the bloody fingerprints now smearing its screen, she raised the phone and turned, scanning the basement with its sharp LED light.

Sister Beatrice appeared instantly in the beam, winking eerily. *"Mum's the word."*

Felix steadied himself and stood upright again, short of breath, ribs inflamed. "Stand firm therefore, having girded your loins with truth, and having put on the breastplate of righteousness, and having shod your feet with the gospel of peace..."

Sister Beatrice turned with pure malevolence and sprang at Felix, slicing at him with the tile knife as he threw his arms across his face to protect himself, still chanting.

"In addition to all, taking up the shield of faith with which you will be able to extinguish all the flaming arrows of the evil one!"

The ghostly nun slashed left and right, spewing protestations and threats in a crazed dance of sickness and possession. *"Hold your tongue, little altar boy! Devil's spawn! Telling secrets! They're ours to keep! For no one else to know!"*

With arms shielding his chest and face like a boxer, Felix pressed on. "And take the helmet of salvation, and the sword of the Spirit, which is the word of God!"

Again, Beatrice struck at Felix, who buckled back and collapsed to the floor for a third time.

Kneeling on the concrete only feet away, Liz aimed her light into the depths of the basement hallway, catching the massive form of Andrew uncomfortably close.

He glared down at Liz, Audrey's head still clamped behind his massive arm.

Liz lowered her stance, left arm throbbing, spattering blood onto the concrete. She lowered the phone into the left breast pocket of the flannel shirt with the light poking from the top, facing outward. "Let her go! Audrey..."

As he released Audrey's arm and reached his left hand out to grab her, Liz fell to the floor and scrambled through his legs into the corridor, shredding her right hand on more debris. Blood oozed from her wounds, staining the flannel shirt a deep crimson and smearing the dusty floor as she crawled, every point of contact a blast of raw agony.

Felix staggered to his feet again, reciting pieces of the Rite of Exorcism from memory. It had been over fifteen years since he'd used any of these holy texts, but there was no better time than the present to pull them out again. "We drive you from us, whoever you may be, unclean spirits, all satanic powers, all infernal invaders, all wicked legions, assemblies and sects! In the Name and by the power of Our Lord Jesus Christ!"

Liz rose, bleeding from both arms, casting the small beam of light back and forth in a furious search for her daughter. "Audrey!"

Immediately she caught them: Andrew, holding Audrey as before, Sister Beatrice standing beside her terrified form, tile knife dangerously close to the young girl's throat.

"Children who tell secrets should be punished." The knife traced a soft line up Audrey's cheek.

Liz reached out a bloody hand. "Please. Don't."

"I told them not to go down there. Naughty boys."

Liz struggled to compose herself. Gathering every ounce of will, she focused on Beatrice, mother to mother. "Sarah, please..."

At the mention of her given name, Sister Beatrice froze perfectly still, eyes wide. The glowing embers faded.

Liz noticed the change and softened her tone. "Sarah. It's not your fault."

The spectral nun shuddered, and began to tremble.

"What your father did to you. It wasn't your fault. No more secrets. We know what he did." Liz swallowed her terror and slowly crept toward the ghostly forms holding her daughter hostage. "Please... you can stop this."

The ghost of Sarah Hurst wavered and swelled with tremors. Something began to disengage, but then the oppressive presence, the amorphous entity that had haunted Felix in the Iraqi desert more than a quarter century ago, came rushing back with a vengeance.

The ember eyes of the demon Eligos blinked open and Sister Beatrice pounced again, but Felix threw his body between them, waving Liz forward.

"Get Audrey!"

The ghostly nun swiped at Felix with the tile knife, striking savagely, driving Felix back into the shadows.

"NO ONE TO KNOW! NO—ONE—TO—KNOW!"

Liz approached Andrew, arms outstretched, the cold brightness of the phone's LED peeking out of the flannel shirt pocket, illuminating his grim face.

"Sarah. She...made you keep her secret, didn't she?" Liz shuddered at the thought of the torments the brute had been subjected to at the hands of his own mother, but her tone was firm. "Let Audrey go, Andrew."

Andrew's filthy face, once wild-eyed and horrible, now almost pitiful, stared back at Liz. He blinked, a look of pain and self-awareness flashing across his face as Audrey struggled against him.

"NO NO NO NO NO!!" Mere steps away, the spectral nun's strikes and swipes became a flurry of savagery. The shredding of fabric and skin could be heard as Beatrice slashed at Felix with superhuman speed and ferocity.

The priest switched his rosary to his left hand, holding it aloft so that the silver crucifix dangled over the edge of his thumb. With his right hand, he grabbed the cuff of his left shirtsleeve and pulled it open, buttons springing and chattering away into the dark. Exposed to the demon's ember eyes was a tattoo of the sigil used from the time of Solomon, to control and banish the entity called Eligos.

"Eligos, Abigor, Eligor," Felix chanted. "I invoke you by name and command you by your own seal, which is inked into my flesh!"

The nun instantly froze as if in some sort of stasis, suspended in midair and mid-strike.

Felix raised his head from its defensive position to address his nemesis from the desert. "These lost souls you inhabit are not your soldiers—they must be judged by Almighty God!"

The ghostly nun's head lowered, mouth open. There it was again—the sound of garbled voices over radio static. The sound his tank crew had heard for weeks in the battlefields of Iraq. The demon was trying to evoke a sense of fear from an earlier time—a powerful weapon in its arsenal, but Felix knew to expect it. He continued, undaunted.

"I command you to leave these souls and this place, now and forever!" He clutched his rosary in front of him, displaying both the silver crucifix and the ancient seal. "Behold this seal of Solomon! See the cross of the Lord! Begone, you hostile powers!"

The ember eyes rolled back in Sister Beatrice's head and she grunted as if in pain, but the sound came from the very beams and rafters. With a shudder, she leaped away into the dark.

Liz, still focused on the brute clutching Audrey, leveled her most serious, motherly look at the ghost of Andrew Hurst. "Let. Her. Go."

Audrey saw the flashlight reflect off the dog tags dangling from her mother's bloody hands. She ducked down, slithering like a reptile out of Andrew's grasp and running to her mother's side.

The hulking janitor, perhaps conceding Audrey's escape, disappeared back into the shadows.

Liz held Audrey tightly, despite the hot twinges of pain emanating from her hands and her right knee. She turned with the phone light to the last place she'd seen Father Felix—

—only to be startled by the livid face of Sister Beatrice in the beam once again. Her flesh was carved in bloody scripture, eyes aglow with demonic power.

"NO ONE TO KNOW!"

She raised the knife to strike at Liz, and Felix blocked the ghostly arm with his own shredded jacket sleeve, rosary coiled around his wrist. The crucifix at its terminus glimmered in the light from Liz's phone, reflecting in the baleful eye of the demonic spirit. The sigil on his inner arm seared into its vision.

"See the cross of the Lord! Begone, you hostile powers!"

Liz raised her own bloody hand, displaying the rosary wrapped around her wrist. "See the cross of the Lord! Begone, you hostile powers!" she repeated.

Father Felix stepped in to join the women facing Sister Beatrice, making the Sign of the Cross in front of him, dispelling the evil presence. "Sarah Hurst, I cast thee out! Andrew Hurst, I cast thee out! Unholy spirits, I cast thee out!" Again he made the Sign of the Cross. "Eligos, Duke of Hell, I cast thee out!"

The creature snarled, a predator wounded and forced into exile. The priest made a final benediction: *"In nomine Patris et Filii et Spiritus Sancti! Amen!"*

"Amen," cried Liz.

"Amen," Audrey repeated, mother and daughter crossing themselves.

There was an unnatural groan as light exploded around them, with a strange rush of ethereal wind and screams of anguish as the restless souls were banished. Father Felix staggered against the spiritual forces whipping around them, and Liz and Audrey fell to the ground, each clutching the other like a life vest. Felix's flashlight spun and skittered to rest by the boiler. All three tensed as the world collapsed in on itself.

The basement fell quiet.

Sister Beatrice was gone. Andrew was gone. The sheet-covered bodies were gone. The blood spatters, all traces of the Edgerton twins, were gone.

Father Felix lowered his arms, squinting around in the darkness. He checked his body for wounds and found his clothes strangely undamaged. He turned around, straining to see Liz and Audrey through the dark. Scuffling to the boiler, he retrieved his flashlight and shined it around the basement.

An uneven patch of concrete, shades lighter than the rest of the floor, lay just behind the rusty boiler. Felix made a mental note of its location, and turned to pan the light over the mother and child behind him.

They opened their eyes and squinted up at the priest. Liz maintained a tight embrace on Audrey, still clutching the dog tags in one bloody hand, her rosary in the other.

Audrey finally spoke. "Mom?"

"I'm here, sweetie," Liz said, not letting go of her daughter.

"They're gone," Audrey announced, as if the most normal thing in the world.

"Yes, honey," Liz nodded, nuzzling Audrey's hair. "They're all gone."

The priest approached from the corner of the basement, scanning them with his flashlight. "Are you alright? Liz, your arm..."

"I'll be okay," she insisted.

Felix extended a hand, and Liz let him help them up. He offered a hand to Audrey and she immediately grabbed him in a tight hug.

"What was all this?" Liz asked.

Felix pursed his lips thoughtfully. "Secrets, Liz. Secrets revealed."

"Can we get out of here, Father?" she sighed.

"Ladies first." The priest aimed his flashlight toward the steps to the exterior door, and three exhausted people trudged toward the stairs, as the wail of emergency sirens began to drift in from outside.

They hadn't worn the uniform or flown the flag of any nation, but they'd been soldiers. Warriors. Defeaters-of-evil.

CHAPTER 19

As night transitioned to dawn, flashing police and EMT lights illuminated the school playground. The crow returned to the cedar tree across the street from the school, watching the goings on and cawing occasionally.

Liz leaned against the Jeep, huddled in an EMT blanket and sipping from a paper cup of coffee with her bandaged hands. She'd taken acetaminophen in preparation for when the lidocaine wore off. Audrey slumbered soundly in the back seat, Father Felix's jacket over her, Jason's dog tags around her neck.

Faye Phillips stood beside Liz, having watched the police go into the basement boiler room. "It's just unbelievable. All this time, right in the basement..." she marveled.

Howard Stonewall, in a vintage tracksuit, paced in a tiny circle near the front of the Jeep. "Incredible," he muttered, shaking his head.

Liz hummed a simple affirmation as she took a sip from her coffee. "Mmm."

"I wonder if they'll find anything," Faye pondered.

"They will," Liz said without a thought. All eyes turned to look at her. She softened her tone and took another sip of coffee, casting a downward look at the pavement. "Pretty sure they will."

Faye moved closer to Liz and tried to make her sincerity known. "It's just so incredible, that you and Audrey figured out this old...tragedy. I'm so sorry for doubting you."

Just then, Father Felix emerged from the basement, ducking under the crime scene hazard tape across the stairwell. In less than a minute, he'd cleared the playground and approached the group. Liz handed him a cup of coffee from the roof of the car.

"Ah. Thank you," said the priest, sipping tentatively from the paper cup.

Several seconds of silence passed before Faye spoke up. "Don't keep us hanging, Father."

Father Felix blinked, remembering where he was. It had been a long night. "Oh, uh...two skeletons. Male, pre-teens. Buried in the corner, behind the boiler."

Faye gasped. "Oh my!"

Liz smiled through tears of trauma. "You found them..."

The priest nodded at the little girl asleep in the car. "Audrey found them. You both found them."

The school quad and parking lot pulsed with red and blue flashes of light from police and emergency vehicles as daylight approached. Somewhere several houses away, a lone dog barked.

☙

Two weeks later.

The old brick Tudor at the end of the street in rural Slaughter County had been packed and loaded onto another moving truck headed south. The October day was sunny but crisp, as Liz and Audrey crammed the family Jeep with the last of the moving boxes and a few loose things they couldn't fit into the moving van.

Audrey finally planted herself on the front steps, cold hands pulled inside the stretched arms of her black hoodie. She read quietly from her comic book, earbuds in, blasting "Escape from Hellview" by CKY.

Liz, in ponytail, USMC t-shirt and jeans, shoved one final box into the back of the Grand Cherokee and returned to the front porch as Sandra emerged from the house, finishing a phone call.

"That's great. Oh that's perfect! Thank you! Okay...mmmhmm...buh bye!"

Liz squinted into the bright noonday sky. "Thank you so much for everything."

"I'm sorry to see you go, but luckily the couple who were looking at the house before you made your offer are still interested. Win-win!"

They shared a quick moment and hug.

"Well, I think that's everything," Sandra said, tears wetting her mascara. "Please keep in touch—let me know when you make it back to San Diego."

Father Felix appeared at the front walk and approached the house.

Sandra noticed him and decided to make her exit. "You have a visitor," she winked at Liz.

"Good afternoon, Father!" Sandra chirped as she passed Felix, heading to her car.

"Sandra…"

Liz watched from the porch. Audrey stood to join her mom as the priest graced their home one last time.

Felix nodded at the full Jeep. "So the rumors are true."

Liz smiled. She looked happy. At peace. There was a healthy pink in her cheeks for the first time since Jason's death. "The rumors are true. Heading back home."

Felix ambled to a stop just feet from Liz and Audrey, squinting in the afternoon sunlight. "As your priest, I feel I must ask—you sure about this?"

Liz's smile broadened, but she nodded wistfully. "Yeah. Yeah, it's good." *As your priest,* she thought. *If only…*

Felix squinted under the brim of the black fedora. "Just want to make sure you're not running away again."

"Nah," Liz assured him. "We finished what we started here. A wise man once told me, 'no way out but through.' And we'll work through it in a familiar place, with family and friends."

She closed her eyes, touching the crucifix around her neck. She felt Jase's warmth lean in next to her, felt his arm wrap around her waist. She opened her eyes, and the sensation was gone. "I'd rather live with the ghosts I know."

"Well you're always welcome in my parish, Mrs. Charles." He glanced down to get Audrey's attention. "You too, Miss Charles."

Audrey reached out to Father Felix, and he swept her up in a great bear hug.

"Thank you, Father," Audrey whispered against his cheek.

"Thank *you*, Audrey."

There was nothing more to say. Felix released Audrey and ambled away from the house, waving as he went.

Liz pulled Audrey to her side, kissing her head. The young girl leaned her head lovingly on her mother's arm, her hand closing around the dog tags hanging from her neck.

"Can I drive?" she asked, fully expecting the look of disbelief that fell across Liz's face.

"Don't push it, kiddo."

They shared a laugh, each aware that the question would become less amusing as time went on and Audrey accelerated into her teen years.

They took a last look at the house, with its rectangular picture window overlooking the dead lawn and the arbor. The sound of seat-belts clicking into place was simultaneous.

The black Jeep pulled out from in front of the old brick Tudor. Liz steered the vehicle onto highway 16 toward Tacoma and points south.

Where the sun was.

THE END

ABOUT THE AUTHOR

Todd Downing's love affair with genre storytelling dates back to his consumption of classic radio dramas and comic books as a child in the 1970s, which broadened into a general appreciation for sci-fi and fantasy media of all kinds.

He grew up in the greater San Francisco Bay Area, writing and drawing from a young age, his works ever-present in school literary journals and newspapers, and eventually on film. He married his high school sweetheart and moved to Seattle in 1991 where he began to write professionally, and worked as an artist in the videogame industry until his publishing company became a full-time operation, while raising two children amid the chaos.

Downing is the primary author and designer of over fifty roleplaying titles, including *Arrowflight, Grimmworld, Airship Daedalus*, and the official *Red Dwarf* RPG. He continues to write genre fiction for stage, film, comics, audio, and adventure gaming products.

Widowed to cancer in 2005, Downing remarried in 2009 and currently lives in a three-generation household in Port Orchard, Washington, with his wife, daughter, mother-in-law, four rescued cats, and a flock of unruly chickens.

Join the author's mailing list:
www.todddowning.com

Thrilling pulp adventure!
www.airshipdaedalus.com

Read the adventures of the Airship *Daedalus:*
A Shield Against the Darkness (Book #1)
*Assassins of the
Lost Kingdom* (Book #2, by E.J. Blaine)
The Golden City (Book #3)
Legend of the Savage Isle (Book #4)
The Arctic Menace (Book #5)
Raiders of the Red Storm (Book #6)

Plus:

AEGIS Tales
A Retro-Pulp Anthology, Volumes 1 & 2

Primordial Soup Kitchen
A Collection of Short Strangeness

Calico Kids

AVAILABLE NOW
in ebook and print!